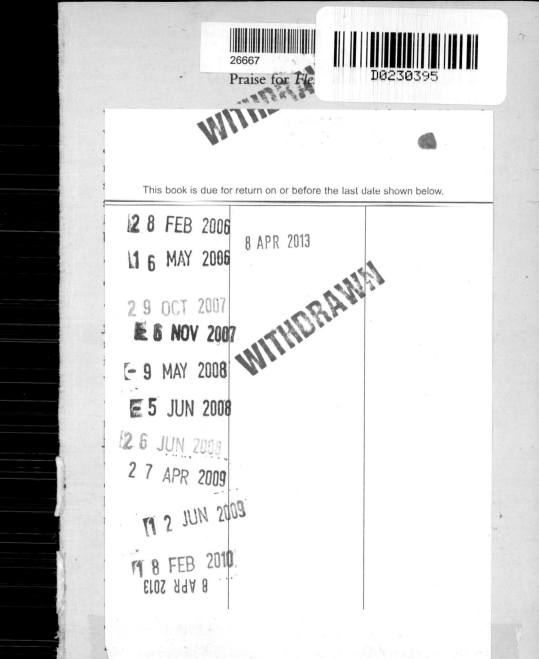
Praise for *Fle*

through. She writes with the adjectival flourish of someone who really does seem to delight in words, who seems able to effortlessly fine-tune them for effect.' *David Robinson, The Scotsman*

Praise for *Mondays Are Red*

'...a stunning, extraordinary debut.' *The Sunday Herald*

'...The challenge for the author is to recreate Luke's heightened perceptions and experiences through words alone and she does so with tremendous style and skill. An outstanding novel that rewards rereading.' *Lindsey Fraser, The Guardian*

'This startlingly original novel explores the power of language and uses words in a remarkable way. A challenging read for young adults.' *Best Book Guide, Book Trust*

'...oddly brilliant.' *The Sunday Telegraph*

'The novel is packed with vivid imagery and startling turns of phrase, and the confusion and inner turmoil of the central character is very well depicted...a memorable novel with an exciting climax.' *The School Librarian*

'...a novel to brood over, written by a new and original talent.' *Nicholas Tucker, The Independent*

'This is an interesting and beautifully written first novel.' *Narinder Dhami, Writer's News*

'...a brilliant adaptation of the Faustian legend...Nicola Morgan is a fresh and original voice for this age group.' *The Bookseller*

'The amazing world of the synaesthate is brought to life in this creative, disturbing and highly original tale from a super new children's author...a thought provoking and fascinating read that will appeal to those aged 13 to adult. *The Children's Bookcase Review*

A division of Hodder Headline Limited

Sleepwalking

NICOLA MORGAN

*Hodder
Children's
Books*

A division of Hodder Headline Limited

Copyright © 2004 Nicola Morgan

First published in Great Britain in 2003
by Hodder Children's Books

A Catalogue record for this book is available
from the British Library

ISBN 0 340 87733 2

Typeset in Bembo by Avon DataSet Ltd,
Bidford-on-Avon, Warwickshire

Printed and bound in Great Britain by
Bookmarque Ltd, Croydon, Surrey

The paper and board used in this paperback by Hodder Children's
Books are natural recyclable products made from wood grown in
sustainable forests. The manufacturing processes conform to the
environmental regulations of the country of origin.

Hodder Children's Books
A Division of Hodder Headline Limited
338 Euston Road
London NW1 3BH

To Hannah and Rebecca,
The brightest future
With all my love

Also by Nicola Morgan

Mondays Are Red
Fleshmarket

Part One

A Story

It was the best of times, it was the worst of times,
it was the age of wisdom, it was the age of foolishness . . .
it was the season of Light, it was the season of Darkness,
it was the spring of hope, it was the winter of despair . . .
A Tale of Two Cities by Charles Dickens

1

A clean space, a room without windows to an outside world. The swan-white walls soothing. The wet-look floor smooth and cool as ancient marble. The ceiling spotted with starry lights and tiny swivelling cameras like flies' eyes. The suck and blow of an air-purif system. Way away in another distance, the tiny bubbled sound of voices. A hum of electricity. The smell of white.

Two women. Each with a baby. Content. Waiting patiently as if for something ordinary.

'What's yours?'

'Plumber.'

'That's nice.'

'What's yours?'

'Caterer.'

'That's nice.'

'How much yours weigh?'

'Four point one.'

'That's nice.'

'Yours?'

'Three point two.'

'That's nice.'

'You got any others?'

'Nah. Smy first.'

'Cool.'

'You got others?'

'Yeah. Two. Nurse and biotechnic.'

'Cool.'

The two women looked down at their babies and made hushing noises, though there was nothing to hush. Each put a clean pink finger in her silent smiling baby's mouth and the baby sucked druggily, its eyes like twin whirlpools. High in the ceiling the hum of the air-purif lulled them all. Warm. Womb-like warm with muggy sapping air. They wriggled to remould the squishtic of their electro-wheelchairs. Set into the left arm of each chair was a small display screen. Both chairs showed red lights. The women must stay where they were until the light showed green and instructions appeared.

One woman lifted her arm slightly and stroked the hair from her baby's forehead. Her arm moved sluggily. She still wasn't used to the small box strapped to it, a thin plastic tube snaking from the box into a vein just inside her elbow. She looked at the LCD on the box.

Pointless to ask what all the lights and lines meant. The woman in the bed next to hers in the Postnatal Center had asked and a nurse had given her some complicated answer about vitarhythms and lobal activity. The woman was odd anyway. It was something in the way she talked, something in the way she bit her lip and her eyes shone with . . . something.

Funny that when you were at home they trusted you to take your daily pim dose – and your funk if you needed something extra. But as soon as you came into a Medicenter they suddenly assumed you were incapable and fixed you up with a box connected to your arm. Not that it bothered her. Not that it bothered anyone. Not that anything bothered anyone. Or anyone who had any sense. There were some weird people out there who bothered about things, she knew. Had seen a prog about it on the digi once. But she didn't bother about them. Bother, bother, why bother? She smiled softly to herself as the tube pumped a drip more something into her veins. She could tell they'd added funk to her dose, too. She could tell by the lovely cotton-wool feeling in her head. Nice.

An invisible door at one end of the white space slid open. Another mother, another wheelchair. It swished towards them. The first woman recognised her – that weird one from the next bed to hers in the Postnatal

Center. There was a strange little fear in the new woman's eyes, a tiny frown. Why would she frown? wondered the other two women. They didn't wonder about it for long. Too much effort.

The wheelchair breathed to a halt nearby.

'Hello,' said the new woman, nervously. And then, 'Oh, hello,' again, with a sudden desperate smile of recognition, as she looked at the face of the first woman.

'Hello,' they said, looking back down at their babies, retreating into their whirlpool eyes and inhaling their warmth.

'How long will we have to wait, do you think?' asked the newcomer.

'Till a green light comes,' said one woman, not looking up.

'But, how long do you think that will be?' Silence. 'How long have you been waiting?'

'Dunno. 'Bout ten. Din't look, din't I?'

There was a buzz. 'Smee,' said one of the first two women, as the green light began to flash on her wheelchair. She looked at the screen and read out loud, slowly, 'Go . . . thru . . . door . . . on . . . left.' And there was an arrow to indicate the direction, in case she had forgotten. But in any case, a door to her left had slid open. A nurse stood there, smiling. With one finger on the touch screen on her right armrest, the woman manoeuvred her chair through this door and disappeared. The door slid closed behind her and became invisible again.

In the humming silence, the newcomer and the other woman looked at their babies. The babies lay, eyes open, peaceful except for twitching lips and tiny butterfly muscle movements in their foreheads and cheeks. Neither had cried. Each had a tiny plastic box strapped to its arm, a thread-thin clear tube slipping inside a whisper of a vein.

The newcomer, Merrilee, spoke. 'Is this your first?'

'Third.'

'Boy or girl?'

'Girl. Caterer.'

Merrilee was silent. She bit her lip and her forehead creased. She knew what she really wanted to ask, but she knew she could not. It was too dangerous.

It was a problem of hers, this needing to question. It had almost got her into trouble countless times when she had to come into contact with the Citizens. If the Governators knew what went on in her head, they could re-prog her and then she would end up like the other Citizens. Well, almost like them. At least taking her daily pim to keep everything in order. Pim – Personality Improvement Medication. A cocktail of brain-altering chemicals individually designed to keep personality faults under control. Too aggressive? Get your pim altered. Too passionate? Get your pim altered. Bored? Get your pim altered. Different? Just alter your pim.

But what was wrong with that, Merrilee wondered? The Citizens were happy, weren't they? Would it be so bad to be happy like them? For a moment she wished she could just give in. Give herself up, go to a medic and just say, 'Look, there's something wrong in my head. I am an Outsider and I don't want to be. Please put it right. I want to come back inside your world and be a good Citizen.'

But no! How could she think like this? It must be the trauma of giving birth. All her natural hormones would be spinning. She imagined her body like a champagne bottle. She could taste the fizz on the tip of her tongue, feel the crackle as it cascaded over the back of her throat. She smiled secretly. These others – they might think they were content, but they couldn't feel like this. They had no words for fizz and froth and champagne and tingle crashing zingle bubble jingle spangle spindle spinning. No word for joy.

That's nice. That's not nice. That was all. And even then it wasn't *real*. What was the point of a world where even nice was not real?

She knew what she wanted to ask the other woman:

'And is this what you want? Knowing now what your tiny baby will become? Do you mind that your child will have no hopes and dreams? Wouldn't you like to wonder? Wouldn't you like your baby to grow up free?'

But she did not ask, because caterer, nurse, plumber, biotechnic, learning facilitator, solatrain driver, food designer – it didn't matter to the other woman. You didn't choose and you didn't dream. Every baby was allocated its future job just after birth, according to what the computer said would be needed in sixteen years' time.

This was what the woman was waiting for now: shortly after birth, a tiny computer chip, no bigger than half a grain of saccharine dust, must be inserted painlessly into every baby's brain, to strengthen and grow the necessary skills, so that the baby would be quite brilliant at its future job. Quite useless at other things, but what did that matter? We enjoy doing what we are good at. Everyone would live happily ever after.

So, this programming was what the woman was waiting for – and Merrilee was supposed to be waiting for it, too. But there was something else. Something worse. Their babies must also be de-languaged. Even the word was ugly, thought Merrilee. De-languaged. But it was compulsory amongst all the Citizens. They had been taught that it was essential for happiness.

Each new baby must have a second tiny chip inserted into its brain, no bigger than a hundredth of a blue poppy seed. It would be placed in part of the language centre in the left half of the brain. This chip would prevent creative language developing. Stories, poetry, rhyme, metaphor, inner meanings, control, the power to invent worlds, deception, wonder, imagination – all would be stopped. Because these things are bad. They are Very Bad Things.

This was the best way. It was the way society worked, for the good of everyone.

And why was this the best way? Because, long ago, it was taught, people had used language to steal power over each other, to deceive, abuse, confuse, and generally cause unhappiness. It had been an unfair world, where some people had this creative power and others didn't. With their clever books and deep poetry and many-layered stories they had made the others feel ignorant. So the Governators said. The powerful ones had learnt ancient dead languages and used the magic power of extraordinary words to create imaginary worlds inside people's heads. Sometimes they had used this power of language to twist the thoughts of others. But the Governators loved their Citizens and wanted to protect them, so they found a way to stop this unfair behaviour.

Better to take this power of language away from everybody, they said. That would be fair. So they invented de-languaging. Now, the Citizens were left with simple words and sentences with simple meaning. Only what was needed to help their lives run smoothly. Because when our lives run smoothly and we have food and warmth and homes and medicine and entertainment and people to care for us, we are content. What more could we need?

That's nice. That's not nice. That's all.

And it worked beautifully. Usually.

Just occasionally something would go wrong. Some people don't have their language centres on the left side of their brain and so the chip might be placed wrongly. Or it might be faulty and lose its power too early. But it made little difference in the end – those children would be identified when they started at Learnacy Center. There was a simple test on entry. Rows of two-year-olds, all tested on day one of Primary Learnacy Center.

Medical staff would attach electrodes to the children's heads. The children didn't mind. They were used to it from routine visits to Medicenters. Once they were all wired up to a central testing unit, the learnacy facilitator would begin, reading in a gentle singsong up-and-downy sort of voice which the children would never

11

have heard before. It was called a story voice. From the old days when there were stories.

'Once upon a time, in a faraway neverland, lived a beautiful princess. Her hair was as long as the sound of honey. Her skin was cake-warm. She smelt of biscuit and caramel and her eyes were lemonade bright. One day, a butterfly, its wings as blue as the sound of sadness, landed gently on her shoulder. "O princess," it whispered, its voice as light as a spider's breath, "I have some terrible news for you."

' "Tell me your terrible news, O butterfly," sang the princess, as she stroked his wings with cloud-soft fingers.

' "Hope is dead. I have searched the world, O princess," replied the butterfly. "I have searched high and low, the murky depths of the deepest ocean and the dizzy peaks of the highest mountain, the furthest sands of the hottest deserts and the iciest reaches of the frozen poles, and I cannot find hope. Hope is dead, O princess. Quite dead." And the butterfly shivered as it cried in the cold empty air.

'The princess smiled again. "Do not fear, gentle butterfly. I have a secret. I am going to have a baby. And in my baby lie all my hopes, all the hopes of the whole wide world. And you will see that we will all live happily ever after because that is the way we will make it be." '

The medical staff watched the monitor of the central testing unit. The learnacy facilitator watched the children as she read. She knew the story off by heart by now. It didn't take an expert to see which children would need to be re-progged. The medical staff could see the unusual activity on the computer screen. The learnacy facilitator could see the excited eyes, the spellbound attention of the problem children. The normal children were fidgeting, bored, this story language passing over them like nothing. But the problem children – oh, those deviant children's brains must be stopped. And fast. Before this strange subversive intrusive ugly weasel snake-slippery language took a hold of them and they became . . . Outsiders.

So the deviant children would be taken in white windowless cars to the nearest Re-prog Center, escorted by Pols. Parental consent was not necessary. The operation must be performed.

Sometimes, unfortunately, even this was not enough. Often these children were left with a strange wispy emptiness somewhere in their brains. These children must learn to take their daily pim, and maybe some funk when things were a little more difficult. If they did this, and attended for regular checks, they might be almost content. They might almost fit in. Specials, they were called. Oh, they were well cared for. They received special education and training and care. But people still looked down on them, while pretending not to.

Merrilee and Ten had both been Specials. Teetering between one world and the next. Until a couple of years ago, when they had made the decision – they had run away and joined the Outsiders for ever.

The price of deserting was enormous. For a start, they had to move from a society where as Citizens all their physical needs were catered for – food, warmth, security, medicine, employment, entertainment – to an underground world of darkness and, often, pain and hunger.

There was also the danger from the police – the Pols. Pols were allowed to shoot Outsiders, as long as there were no Citizens nearby who might see and be upset by such violence. These extreme measures were seen as necessary because occasionally there were outbreaks of neobubonic plague amongst the Outsiders. Although there was never a danger to Citizens with their advanced medicine, nevertheless it was irritating and unhygienic to find dead bodies clogging up the sewers. The biotechnics were working to alter the genetic make-up of the plague bacterium so that it killed the fleas before they could pass it to humans. They had almost succeeded. Meanwhile, it was only sensible to allow the Pols to shoot any Outsiders who happened to be seen on the streets during any plague outbreak.

The Pols enjoyed this and viewed it as sport. Most of their work was routine, dull, in a society where most people were so 'happy' that they didn't bother to commit crime and where behavioural problems were dealt with by pim. Long ago, people had hunted foxes. Today, the Pols hunted people. They performed a service for the City and why should they not enjoy it?

Now Merrilee had a baby. She looked down at the baby's eyes. They were Ten's eyes. There was something deep in there, Merrilee knew. Something worth more than being programmed and orderly. Her heart melted.

Her baby was not going to be programmed. They were to be part of the Poet's plan. Merrilee had never met the Poet, but she had heard of his plan. She didn't know the details – no one did. But she had been told that if she and Ten would hand over their baby when it was born, the baby would be cared for and brought up in safety, away from the dangers and poverty of their underground existence in the City. Their child would be safe, happy, healthy and would grow up to be important, to play a part in the new world, a community of free people. Could her baby be part of such a world? It seemed like a dream, but it was a dream that was better than the hard life amongst the Outsiders.

Especially with the new plague outbreak spreading from the Northern Zone.

But Merrilee's pregnancy had been complicated and for a while it looked as though she might lose the baby. Then, when she had thought nothing could be done, a message had come, from an Outsider called Milton. He was working for the Poet. There were so few babies that her baby had become especially important, and Merrilee must go to a Medicenter. She and Ten were told to travel down to the Center Zone. Milton had made arrangements for her to have a fake ID-chip and for her baby to avoid programming. Now, seeing her baby, her beautiful deep-eyed baby, she didn't think she could go through with it. Could she change her mind? Keep the baby with her? Surely she could bear the hard life of an Outsider better if she had her baby?

She noticed that the other woman was gliding away in her wheelchair towards the door. It slid shut behind her.

Alone in the clean white space, Merrilee sat. She tried to keep the panic down, tried not to bite her lip. Had Ten failed? She could be called at any moment and then her baby would be programmed like the others. Ten had promised that this wouldn't happen. She had only agreed to have her baby in the Medicenter because she had been ill. Normally, Outsiders just had their babies underground and, if they died, they died. Oh, but they had beautiful ceremonies when someone died. People wrote poems, sang songs, made each other cry with ancient stories. They washed their hearts clean with tears. Citizens just took funk or changed their pim dose at their next medicheck.

Could the cameras see through Merrilee's expression? She tried to look blank. Everyone looked the same in here. Dressed in white paper. Trousers, loose and comfortable. So loose and comfortable that you almost felt you weren't wearing anything. A tunic the same. She felt the tiny bump under the skin on her wrist where her fake IDchip had been inserted. The Outsiders had contacts who could arrange this, for a price.

What if Ten had failed? What if he were too late? Merrilee's heart was pounding. Her skin was sweating. Instinctively she put her hand on her arm, where the plastic box was taped. She fingered the tube, the tube which was *not* connected to the box which should be delivering her drugs. She had disconnected it. She was tempted, just briefly tempted, to reconnect it and take the peace it offered. But no – better to feel, to suffer, to know what was real.

Bzzzzz. She jumped. Looked up at the cameras guiltily before looking down at her screen. She read the words, aloud and disjointedly, as she knew she had to.

Citizens usually read aloud and in an automatic stilted monotone, disconnected words without expression. She had learnt not to give herself away by reading silently or fluently.

'Due . . . 2 . . . a . . . malfunct . . . in . . . a . . . human . . . resource, . . . ur . . . appt . . . has . . . been . . . rescheduled . . . 4 . . . 2 morrow. Pls . . . proceed . . . thru . . . door . . . on . . . ur . . . right . . . and . . . return . . . 2 . . . ur . . . allocated . . . bed.'

Ten had done it! Oh, how she wanted to see him! She clenched the muscles of her mouth to stop a grin spreading all over her face, kept her gaze staring downwards, away from those cameras, as she manoeuvred the wheelchair whispering through the now-open door. A nurse with silent squishtic-innered shoes led her along the corridors back to her bed in Bloc Daffodil of the Postnatal Center.

2

An orderly took her baby while she climbed back into bed. The nurse took her arm. 'What's this? Didn't you notice this had come out?'

'Sorry,' said Merrilee. 'No, I didn't notice.' She kept her voice level. The nurse attached it again, giving it an extra little push just to make sure. Merrilee tried to will the liquid not to enter her body, tried to breathe above it, but it didn't work. Back came the familiar schizo world of being content and yet knowing there was something not to be content about. She knew, or she had been told, that real Citizens felt properly content, that they did not even know they had lost their freedom.

She longed for a world where they could all be free. If her baby could be part of that . . .

But she felt too weak, a dizzy meltingness flooding up from her toes, sucking her strength and will. She just wanted to stay here. She was so tired.

The orderly had gone. Her baby! She tried to sit up but her muscles were weak. Panic in her lungs, her breath fluttering, her words trapped. 'My baby! I want my baby!' Other heads turned slowly towards her, mildly interested, looking from above their knitting, their fingers hovering over the careful stitches, the tap tap sounds suddenly silent. She had not noticed the tap tap sounds until they had stopped. Or the digi in the corner, pulsing tinnily into the women's ear-pieces.

The nurse put her hand on Merrilee's shoulder. In a loud voice, slow and clear, she said, 'Your baby has been taken for a test. A routine test. It is normal for you to worry. You have just given birth. I will add something to your pim, a little more funk to help you along.' As she leant towards Merrilee, the white smell of her warmed into a drifting honeysuckle cloud. Their eyes met. 'Don't worry about your baby,' whispered the nurse. 'Remember the story of Pandora? What was left in the box after Pandora had tipped all the evil into the world? It was hope. Your baby carries the hopes of all the world on her shoulders.'

'You? You are an . . . ?'

'No,' whispered the nurse, as she pretended to tuck the sheets tightly around Merrilee's bed. 'Not an Outsider,' she said. 'I'm a nurse. But I chose to be a nurse. I wasn't programmed. My parents are Outsiders. I was born underground. My mother teaches writing and my father is a poet. But I wanted to be a nurse. Couldn't handle the life of an Outsider − living underground? Me! Too cold. Dirty. Besides,' she shrugged, 'I couldn't get all that latin and grammar. I just wanted to be a nurse. So I gave myself up. Became a Citizen. And it means I can . . . er . . . control my own pim, if you know what I mean?'

'You mean not take it?'

'Or take it, whichever. Or take something different. Depends what effect I want. See? I am one of them, one of the ordinary, obedient ones. Proper little Citizen, to look at me! But I can use my brain when I want to – I wasn't programmed at birth, remember? Late programming never works properly. I used to know the Poet when I was younger, you know. He even taught me to write poetry, a little bit. Just in my head, just for myself. That's why I'm helping you and Ten. And there's something about that baby. I can see it in her eyes.'

And she was gone. Leaving behind her the honeysuckle warmth, her electricity, her humanness. Merrilee closed her eyes, in case she was being watched. She breathed deeply and slowly, fighting to slow her heart. Where was her baby? She had to trust Ten. And the nurse.

But she wanted her baby with her.

She looked down at the box on her arm. The tube was detached again. It must have been the nurse.

She turned her eyes away from the ward, the knitting

21

women, the flying fingers, the constant glitz from the digi. Through the windows, Merrilee could see the moon already. No stars, the darkness too dirtied by lights, too yellow. It was a long time since she had seen stars.

Where was Ten? When would he come? Would they be strong enough? And where was her baby now?

Later, she must have slept, because into her sleep came gentle hands wakening her. The nurse. A light shining in her face. Her bed began to slide out of the dark quietness of the ward with the humming of machines and the whishing of sleeping mothers' breaths. No crying of babies. Babies were in the Newb-Center. Having nocturnal tests for this and that. Having any genetic imperfections corrected.

Now she was being wheeled faster, along corridors quiet and empty. Past the occasional wheezing vaku-cleaner. She looked up at the dimmed lights on the ceiling as she glided along. She felt like a planet being spun on its orbit through the stars. Faster and faster sang the sliders and she pulled the covers tightly up around her chin and wished she could fall asleep and not have to go through what she knew was coming. If only she could sleep and wake as someone else.

'Merrilee!' His voice came from a distance and she twisted her head to see him.

'Ten!' And her bed stopped moving as he took her in his arms and hugged and hugged her limp body and suddenly she felt real again. Strong and alive.

'Oh Ten! Where is she? Where's our baby?'

'She's coming, Merri. They're bringing her. What is she like?'

'She's beautiful! She's so soft. Her hair smells of biscuits and her skin is warm as . . . oh, I don't know, but just wait till you touch her. There's something in her eyes, Ten. Her eyes are kind of like stars, but brighter. But how did you do it, get us away in time?'

'It doesn't matter now. And it's not over yet. There's a place we have to take her. Milton will meet us and then . . .' He held her as she shook.

'I don't know if I can, Ten!'

'I know, Merri. I know. I don't know if I can either, but we have to. If there's any chance of giving her the best life, we have to do it. She'll be safe and happy and she can make something of her life, really make something. She can be free. Think of that!'

'Hurry,' urged the nurse, looking around her nervously.

'Can you walk?' asked Ten.

Merrilee tried to sit. Dizziness came in starbursts. But she could manage. If they would only bring her baby.

And then the smell of milky biscuits and there was her baby, carried in an orderly's arms, gently, as if she really mattered. Merrilee took the bundle in her arms and showed her baby to Ten. His eyes swam and shone.

He turned to Merrilee. 'I love you,' he said. 'Whatever happens. I love you and it was worth it.'

She smiled. 'How much do you love me?' It was their old routine, the one they used to remind themselves that they were now Outsiders, and why it was good to be so.

'As much as the stars in the sky and the bubbles in a sea of champagne.'

'As much as the ripples of sand in a desert storm and the petals in a rose tornado.'

'More than the souls that have been and the souls that will be.'

'More than all the ideas ever thought and all the thoughts never spoken.'

'Go now,' said the nurse. 'Hurry!' They slipped through the door and out into the night. 'Good luck!' called the nurse quietly. The door closed behind them. They were alone, the three of them, for the first time.

They hurried to the row of solacars and Ten put coins in the slot. The door of the first car slid open and Ten helped Merrilee in. Clutching the baby tight, she wriggled herself comfortable on the squishtic seats and fastened the harness. Her heart danced as Ten manoeuvred the car slowly onto the cartrak and then sped away. The three of them. Together.

Soon the striped solon lights and people sliding along moving glass-covered walkways gave way to darker streets. Derelict old-fashioned shops with silver wire grilles protecting them. Few people ventured here at night – not because it was dangerous, just because there was no entertainment.

Eyeless automated tanks washed the pavements and a man lying in the gutter was soaked by the green spray. An Outsider dropout, perhaps, drunk on home-made wine. It was part of the Pols' work to deal with such eyesores, but they had obviously missed this one. The black strips of buildings sped past, silently. At first when she looked up through the thick plastic roof, Merrilee thought she could see stars but soon she realised it was only the lights in moonscrapers, most more than a hundred and fifty floors high. She was looking up through the maze of walkways and solatrain tubes that criss-crossed the air between the buildings.

Looking down again, Merrilee placed her baby in the built-in baby-carrier. 'There are some of your clothes in this bag, Merri.' Ten passed the bag he had been carrying back to her. Merrilee rummaged. Unfastening the harness, she wriggled quickly into her own comfortable clothes. There was food in the bag. She passed a bar to Ten and they munched in cosy silence, punctuated by occasional comments and the swishing sounds of passing solacars, fewer now, their windows bright with passengers staring into nothing.

At first, they did not, could not, talk about what was going to happen. But eventually Merrilee had to ask, 'Where are we going, Ten?'

'We are meeting Milton. He will take our baby and she'll go to the Poet with the other babies. She will have a wonderful life, a life of real freedom. She will be free to grow and do all that we can't. We have to do it, Merri.' He spoke as if trying to convince himself.

Merrilee looked into her baby's whirlpool eyes. She gently pulled the tube from the tiny vein and removed the box that was connected to her baby. For a moment the world still spun haphazardly in those new eyes, but after a few seconds, quite suddenly, the meaningless spangles vanished into the depths and instead the clear black pupils glistened. With a trembling of the lips, the baby began to cry. It was the first time Merrilee had heard her cry and her heart dissolved. She picked her up and held her to her breast. The baby looked up and their eyes met, properly for the first time. At that moment, Merrilee's heart began to crack.

Ten looked at the radar. They were at their

destination. He must make sure no Pols were around. When he was as sure as he could be, he slid into a parking bay.

The doors wheezed open. Outside, darkness. Buildings, unlit. No streetlights here. Only the thick yellow greyness from the sky. No people. A scuttling over there, some sort of animal. The jangle of a rolling bottle clattering roughly over broken ancient concrete.

A face appeared at the car door. Outsider. Long coat, patched. Hands dirty, with long strong fingers. Handsome, in a classical way. Wide eyes gleaming with fire. Thick hair, flopping over a high forehead, strong cheekbones, jutting chin. A perfect smile as he greeted Merrilee.

'You must be Merrilee? Milton, at your service. And here is your baby! What are you calling her?'

Merrilee looked at the baby. 'Her name's Hope.'

'How fitting. Let me see her properly.' He looked into Hope's eyes as she lay in her mother's arms. He smiled. 'There is a whole world in those eyes. Now,' and he turned to Ten. 'I have to go. It is dangerous to stay here. It is exactly the sort of place where the Pols go hunting. Let me take her now, Merrilee.' He held out his arms.

How could she do this? The baby was a part of her, hooked into her heart by fingers as old as the world. She would rather die with her baby. The thought of life without her was unbearable.

Ten placed his fingertips on her cheeks, looked into her eyes. 'Merri, we have to do this. It's for Hope. Because she is special.'

She couldn't do it. Something hard and physical stopped her. 'I can't,' she gasped.

Milton looked at her. 'She will be cared for, loved. She will grow up free. Let her go, Merrilee. You are doing it for Hope. But it's for all of us too, for all the Outsiders – for a new future, a free world. We all need her.'

But I need her! she wanted to scream. She couldn't do it. How could anyone? She wanted to take her baby and run with her for ever. But she *must* do it. She knew that. For Hope. For Hope, she repeated into the storm inside her head.

Ten and Merrilee kissed their baby, staring desperately into her clear, deep eyes, touching every bit of her face, her tiny curled fingers, her breath-soft hair. Tears choked Merrilee's heart as Milton took the baby gently from her arms.

The baby gave a small cry and then was quiet as Milton tucked her under his coat and disappeared down a narrow alley. He was gone. How could it have happened so quickly? Could she not have had a little more time? The emptiness was enormous. As huge as space. A space without stars.

Frantically, Merrilee ran after her baby, but almost immediately she felt Ten's hand on her shoulder. He pulled her round and gripped her to him. Merrilee buried her face in his coat. She could not breathe. Could not even cry.

Suddenly the air exploded into light. Shocked, they looked up. A car raced towards them, its headlights blinding, its engine hissing. Three Pols leapt out and stood facing them. All they could see against the dazzling lights were the black silhouettes of tightly-clothed bodies. And the outstretched hands holding something. Guns. They knew without looking.

There was nowhere to run and they clung to each other. Ten pushed Merrilee's face into his shoulder so she could not see what was happening. Would they kill them both? Or would they do something unspeakable to them first? There were rumours that this could happen. He did not want to believe it.

He whispered in her ear. 'Merri, whatever happens, Hope is safe! Remember that!'

'I need my baby!' was all she could say, and her voice began to tangle with the storm in her head.

'I love you and Hope loves you,' he insisted, his lips against her skin.

'How much do you love us?' her smile twisted through her tears. She knew what would happen now and it didn't matter.

He lifted his head and shouted aloud, 'As much as the stars in the sky and the bubbles in a sea of champagne.'

Her heart swelled as she shouted her reply into the air, 'As much as the ripples of sand in a desert storm and the petals in a rose tornado.'

And just before the dull thunks of the bullets as they slammed into his body, she heard him cry, 'More than the souls that have been and the souls that will be.' He crumpled to the ground and she screamed instead of him. Stared wide-eyed at the place where his still body lay like a rag, the trickle of blood already slowing. Inside her head she screamed again but all that came out was a sob.

As she stood there gasping for breath, terrified, a strength came from somewhere buried deep. She clasped her arms around herself, imagining, feeling, her baby's body in the place where she had last held her, and she sank on her knees to the ground.

Her words rose into the sky. 'More than all the ideas ever thought and all the thoughts never spoken.'

The bullets sliced silently into her body and as she fell and as she crumpled and as she span towards the light, Merrilee laughed as she saw all the stars in the universe.

And in the sliver of time before she died, she saw a butterfly shiver from her head and flutter away to keep its secret. That Hope was not dead after all.

Part Two

Balmoral Castle –

Sixteen Years Later

For the secret of human existence does not consist merely in living, but in what one lives for.
The Brothers Karamazov by Fyodor Dostoyevsky

1

As the Poet closed the door to the study, he tried to let his breath out slowly. His heart hammered and his legs felt watery with shock. Could his ambitions be destroyed now? He only needed a few more years. They were so close.

But not now! His work of the last seventeen years would be utterly wasted. He had given up everything for this. He had even lost the woman he loved.

Yet he could not ignore the message he had just received.

The Poet shivered in his thick gnarled jumper, and walked slowly towards a door in the corner of the enormous hall, his kilt swinging. His knee seemed more painful when he had bad news, as if to remind him of his failure all those years ago. He did not need to be reminded.

He passed the dusty portraits of royalty, covered with the grime of generations. They had stopped bothering to clean them long ago. No one had visited this place for many years. Why visit the 'real thing' when the real thing was old and musty and cold and you could visit a virt-reality theme park instead, which would be bright and warm and full of noise and coloured lights and instant food in infinite flavours? But although he might disapprove of this modern habit of virtual entertainment, it did suit his purpose. It meant that no tourists visited the palace of Balmoral any more.

After the removal of the royal family over a hundred years before, Balmoral had become a museum. But it was years since the last tourist had visited and no one from the Government cared that a nearly sixty-year-old man still lived there. They had forgotten him. He was still the curator, as far as the records were concerned. The fact that he was an Outsider had never bothered them – no Citizen should have to endure living in the countryside, at the mercy of the weather and without continual entertainment. The Governators did not know about the children.

The Poet frowned. The children. Or 'young people' as he knew he should call them. The oldest only sixteen years old. They took nothing seriously. Yet the future of the Outsiders was now in their hands.

He hesitated at the door and then opened it. Rows of faces turned towards him, pausing in their meal.

'Who was it? Anyone interesting? Message for me?' asked a girl's drawling voice as she picked something from her teeth. Livia. It would have to be Livia. Her black-rimmed eyes, heavily made-up with liner and a shiny silver streak flashing towards the paper-thin eyebrow, seemed to laugh at him. If anyone were to say anything, it would always be Livia.

'No, Livia, it was not a message for you. Why would it be a message for you?' he asked witheringly. He didn't mean to — it was just that Livia sometimes affected him like that. He often found himself wanting to snap at her, anything to shake her horrible teenage carelessness. She could be so much more than she let herself be. If she ever took life seriously, she could be a star. She hid her brilliance under ridiculous clothes and make-up and moody behaviour, and wasted her talents.

He continued. 'It was, nevertheless, someone interesting. However, I am not at liberty to enlighten you until I have discussed the matter with your teachers.' Why did he always sound so pompous when he spoke to Livia and the others?

'Madame Bovary, Mr Stevenson, Dr Grimm, Mr Cicero, a word with you all, please. Staff room. Boys and girls, you may go outside when you have finished, but stay where you can hear us when we call. Thank you. Please continue.' Without waiting, the Poet left the dining-room and hurried along a threadbare corridor to the staff room. Its enormous windows let in a few rays of thin sunlight. A fire blazed in the grate but the room was still cold. The heating system was the ancient unreliable one from the early twenty-first century. Normally such things were not expected to last, but this one still managed to pulse out weak heat a hundred years later, helped by Lochinvar's ingenuity with anything mechanical.

The other teachers followed the Poet into the room.

'I shall put the coffee-spa on,' said Mr Stevenson, moving elegantly towards the corner. You might almost call it gliding, he moved so smoothly – like a swan, its neck bent coyly. The coffee-spa had been moved from the café when Balmoral ceased to be a tourist attraction. 'Latte, everyone? Skinny for you, I presume, Madame?' They still enjoyed the old-fashioned pleasures here.

Stevenson's tomato-red rollneck jumper was almost the only brightly-coloured object in the room. Apart from the fuschia flash down the sides of Madame Bovary's little nycro jacket and otherwise entirely black, thigh-gripping trousers, or *slicks*. Madame Bovary loved the way the cloth gripped her hips. The material was electrolon, the revolutionary fabric that sent tiny electric currents through the flesh to tone the muscles while the wearer did nothing. She knew the young people sniggered about it – but they would need it one day too, she reassured herself, patting her little stomach.

'Something a little stronger than coffee is called for, I fear,' said the Poet, unlocking a cupboard and pulling out a crusty bottle of something amber.

Dr Grimm was cold. It was always cold in this damned place. He threw another log on the fire and hunched over it, pulling a pipe from his ancient tobacco-coloured jacket and lighting it with a stick from the flames. He sucked slappily on the tooth-worn stem and dragged the smoke into his mouth. At least this so-called emergency had given him an extra free period – any time spent not teaching those revolting teenagers was time spent happily, in his view. He was too old to be teaching brats. And what was the point of it anyway? So, they were brilliant – well, they would be, wouldn't they? They were taught by him, after all. But what was the point? They took nothing seriously. It was all a waste of time. Still, it was better than living underground in the City or in some freezing, crumbling farmyard in the country. That was why he had willingly volunteered to come to Balmoral, eleven years ago now, when the first children were old enough to begin their formal education.

The Poet put the sherry bottle on a table and limped over to a window. He watched the young people meander past, scuffing the gravel. Why didn't they ever move in a straight line? They jostled each other, kicked a ball about, sometimes stumbled, laughed, shouted, stopped walking for no reason. They walked so close, frequently colliding, like molecules of boiling water.

Cicero was looking at him. 'May one assume that you intend to tell us the nature of this emergency?' Cicero's high-domed forehead was wrinkled like a blanket. He could be trusted to take a situation seriously. Mr Stevenson and Madame Bovary also watched the Poet, waiting. Only Dr Grimm did not, staring into the fire and blowing smoke rings gloomily, the corners of his mouth perpetually dragged down.

'Yes, I am afraid I have some rather . . . difficult news.' A thud as a football thwacked against the wall near the window. He winced, his teeth gritted. 'Bloody children,' he snapped.

'But they are only, as you say, children,' said Cicero, peering over his wire spectacles.

'And that, my dear Tullius, is the whole problem. They are only children. The oldest only sixteen years old and yet now, suddenly, they must do the work of adults.'

'What do you mean?' asked Stevenson.

'The message. Bad news. About the sickness in the City, virus, whatever it is – it's worse. Much worse than we imagined. It's . . .' He had to stop. His heart was beating too fast and his legs were water-weak again.

He had their full attention now. Madame Bovary's artificially smooth forehead was creased in a frown. Stevenson stood very still, his lips tight and thin, one eyebrow raised. Cicero waited, wheezing slightly in the smoke from Grimm's pipe. And even Grimm watched the Poet now, his red-veined nose large and pitted, his eyebrows meeting in one bushy black line. The smell of pipe, and firewood, and damp, and ancient books and unwashed clothes filled the air.

'For goodness' sake, I'll, spit it out, why don't you?' urged Stevenson.

'It's not easy,' said the Poet. He took a deep breath. 'First, let's have that sherry. Tullius, will you do the honours?' While Cicero poured a generous measure into five glasses, the Poet began to speak. As he did, his voice became stronger. Everything would work. He must believe it. What was his life without that? The Poet was a man of passion and belief. He was a man who made things work.

'The message was from Milton's daughter. Cassandra. He wants our help. It's the sickness amongst the Outsiders. No one knows what it is or where it has come from, but it's killing them off. Some people die within days, others linger. Some survive, but in a very weakened state, their lungs damaged and their limbs wasted away. Almost half the Outsiders in the Center Zone have died. Many more are ill. They say that other groups in the Northern Zone have been hit just as hard.'

'But what can *we* do about it?' asked Madame Bovary, her perfect nose wrinkling in distaste at the thought of illness and death.

'We have two choices. We can do nothing. But Milton believes they'll be wiped out entirely if this continues. We can't let that happen. They are our people. All of us have relatives, old friends there.'

'And our other choice?' asked Cicero.

'Milton wants us to send some of our young people to the City. Now. To help Cassandra find a way into Center Tower as soon as possible. There's no one left who can help her. The virus has destroyed their will to fight. She would do it on her own, but it's impossible – much too dangerous – and Milton won't let her try. She's all he's got, after all. We always planned that one day our young people would go to the City and find a way to change the system. And we knew that they would have to penetrate Center Tower.'

'Yes, but that was when they were all grown up! That was the plan – *your* plan. They are only sixteen! We *have* to wait – otherwise it's all been a waste of time. We need more of them to be ready and then they can all go together – and not when this sickness is rife. It's too risky! And ridiculous.' Stevenson's face was red. He shook his head in disbelief. He had never been a passionate believer in the plan. The Poet always suspected he was only there to avoid the squalor of life underground.

'We can't wait. If we wait, we lose everything. If all the Outsiders in the City die out, what chance would any of our young people ever have of penetrating Center Tower? They wouldn't survive an hour in the City on their own.' The Poet's jaw clenched in frustration. Why couldn't they see? If he was younger, he would go himself, he thought, ignoring the fact that his damaged knee would not get him far. He looked around the others: two ancient crocks, a spindly man who couldn't run ten metres without wheezing, and a woman who wouldn't last a day without access to her dermoplactive creams.

'Preposterous! Bloody preposterous! What a bloody shambles!' This from Dr Grimm.

'What if the poor children catch the nasty sickness?' asked Madame Bovary.

'They will simply have to be careful. They are strong and healthy – healthier than any Outsiders in the City. And we can get Lochinvar to concoct one of his oils – we've used that before.'

'Yes, for colds! This is somewhat stronger than the common cold! This is a plague! What can Lochinvar's oils do against that?' Stevenson asked.

The Poet glared at him. 'We will just have to hope. For goodness' sake! There is no other way!'

'Should we not go ourselves, PB? We could go with them at least,' said Cicero.

'No, Tullius. We are too old,' replied the Poet. Madame Bovary opened her mouth to speak. The Poet smiled at her. 'With all respect,' he said gently, 'we are not exactly in our prime. Life underground requires physical fitness. The young people are strong, healthy – they will survive.' He paused, now believing it himself. He had their attention. He continued.

'I have dreamt of this moment. Yes, in the words of that hero from history who lived and fought and died for his cause, I have a dream. I dream of a world where the old ways rule again, the ways of truth, of meaning. Where power is in the hands of the people, where an individual can choose his way, her life, where free will reigns. What has happened to this country of ours? Why do the Citizens walk like robots with empty smiling faces? Why do they not question, rebel, fight? Why do they not feel pain or sorrow or fear or anger? And how can they not see that without these emotions there is no real happiness? My dream is a world where people can use their brains again, know the truth. And know how to feel. Pleasure *and* pain.

'And all this is in the hands of our young people, the young people whom we have nurtured since their infancy. We have taught them to use their brains fully. We have trained them in stories, poetry, science, knowledge and thought, so that there is nothing they cannot know and understand. With that power, there is nothing they cannot do.'

'Except that they are not ready.' Cicero pushed the spectacles back up his nose. Though the fire burned, the room felt chilled.

'They must be ready, Tullius. They are all we have. They must find a way to penetrate to the very heart of Center Tower. It will be dangerous, very dangerous, perhaps impossible, but only when they discover how this society works will they be able to find a way to change it.'

Something burned behind his eyes. They would win! They would do what he had wanted to do when he was young. He had dreamed of revolution then. He and some friends used to sit around plotting to overthrow the system, but they could never agree how to do it. And then there had been their failed attempt to raid a Medicenter for drugs to deal with an underground flu outbreak. Many of them had been shot dead by the Pols.

Only he and Milton had survived that disastrous night. Milton had saved his life, dragging him away when the Pols had shot him in the knee. How could he ignore Milton's plea for help now?

'I am sorry, PB,' interrupted Dr Grimm, 'I am sincerely and deeply sorry to have to say this . . .' Grimm did not look sincerely or deeply sorry, shaking his head in contempt and chewing on his pipe between each phrase. '. . . but it really is bloody ridiculous. Absolutely bloody preposterous. They're teenagers, for God's sake. They've got hormones buzzing around like flies on a dog-turd and they're far more likely to have sex with each other the moment we take our eyes off them than save the bloody country! I mean just how exactly do you imagine they are going to change society, as you so quaintly put it?'

'I haven't the faintest idea how they are going to do it,' said the Poet coolly, his voice calm but with something hard in his grey eyes. 'But I know that all they can do, all anyone can *ever* do, is their best. Choices, truth, free will, Grimm – they're worth fighting for. We can't all sit and grumble and cough and splutter every time there's a setback. Some of us choose to act, to fight.'

'Hear, hear! I agree,' cried Madame Bovary, looking at the Poet with passion in her eyes.

'So,' asked Cicero. 'Whom do you propose we send?' They all looked at each other.

'I think just three at first. We don't want to send them all. Any suggestions?' asked the Poet.

There was silence. How did you judge between a bunch of kids who took all the wrong things seriously?

'I'd say Marcus,' said Cicero, 'if we've got to send anybody. He's a bit hot-headed. But he's physically the strongest.'

'And Tavius, do you think?' said the Poet. 'You couldn't call *him* hot-headed.'

'As long as he can summon up the enthusiasm to get out of bed in the morning,' said Stevenson. 'He's so casual he makes me feel sleepy to look at him. He's not a team-player, either. He doesn't form close friendships – how can the others trust him?'

'He'll be calm under pressure,' said Cicero. 'And there's no danger of him being impulsive or emotional. He'll do what's required.' They all nodded. Stevenson shrugged.

'Well, the third has to be Livia,' said the Poet.

Madame Bovary shook her head.

'Too risky,' said Cicero.

'She'll cause problems with her temper,' said Grimm.

'Milton asked for her.' The others looked surprised. 'Why?'

'I have no idea,' replied the Poet. 'He often asks about all the babies he brought here. We talk about them. But he's always been especially interested in Livia. Anyway, I agree with him. She's a natural leader. She has fire. She makes things happen.'

'Of course, if she decides she wants to,' said Madame Bovary. 'But I agree, it is too risky. She is, how do you say, a liability.'

'Livia goes,' said the Poet again. 'I trust her. So does Milton.'

'But . . .'

'No buts. She's going.'

The others were silent. They hoped he was right. Livia would not have been their choice. She was too selfish. She could never control her emotions.

'So, Marcus, Tavius, and Livia – we agree?' said the Poet, looking at them all. What could they say? They had no better suggestions. 'My friends,' he said, 'we should drink a toast.'

'What toast do you propose?' asked Cicero.

The Poet raised his glass.

'To hope!' he said.

'To hope!' they all echoed.

Before their glasses had even reached their lips, there was a huge thud and a yell as a ball crashed into the bars across the window and Livia's voice was heard to shout,

'Get your king hands off me, Marcus!' before she dissolved into screams. The teachers all looked at each other and slowly shook their heads.

'We had better tell them now,' said the Poet. 'I shall fetch them. Meet me in the classroom in ten minutes.' And he left the room, walking awkwardly up the steps and across the hall.

His eye caught the portrait of the last Prince William. While he was still a Prince. Poor boy. Poor boy indeed, he thought, remembering his history. And now 'king' was a swearword, for goodness' sake.

He paused in the open doorway of the office. One wall consisted entirely of a huge screen, divided at the moment into two sections. Lochinvar, a middle-aged wiry man, his face battered by weather till it was the colour of steak, sat near it. His legs, with muscles like metal ropes protruding from under his khaki shorts, were propped on the desk and he whittled a stick with a small knife while reading a battered copy of *The Prince*. On one section of the screen, which made almost no sound because he had turned the volume right down, flashed a dizzying stream of lights and laughing faces and cartoon grins and graphic splats. On the other section was a square window which read, 'u hav 1 . . .' and then a smiling picture of an envelope.

This was their only contact with the City. The

computer, or 'com', had been installed when the castle first became a museum, so that the officials could send instructions to the curator. Although it was by now very old-fashioned, it still worked. The Poet could communicate with the Outsiders in the City through Milton, whose daughter, Cassandra, had access to a com belonging to a Special. It also meant that the children could watch (for educational purposes only, of course) the few digi-channels that came through on the ancient digi-screen linked in the next room. In this way, they could find out much of what was happening in the City. Unfortunately, it also meant they picked up the City slang.

Lochinvar had been born in the castle and lived there all his life, the only one of them all who could claim that. He was descended, through at least four generations, from the chief butler of the Last Prince, when he had been King. King. Lochinvar always let that delicious swearword roll around his tongue like baccy. Now, Balmoral would not run properly if it were not for him and his contacts, and his knowledge of every last solar panel and power wire in the building. It was, some might even say, Lochinvar's castle. Sometimes the Poet had a strange sense of being only a guest. This was ridiculous, of course – it was *his* castle, *his* plan. Everyone knew that.

He didn't go into the office. He decided to leave before Lochinvar was aware of his presence. He preferred not to tell him what was happening yet. Lochinvar was very attached to the young people. He was as much a believer in the plan as anyone. In fact, when the Poet thought about it, he remembered that many of the ideas in the early days had been Lochinvar's as the two of them sat sharing a few malt whiskies in the dark evenings before the others had arrived, Lochinvar wearing the butler's uniform passed down from his father. He still wore it sometimes, on special occasions. That was another of Lochinvar's ideas: that they should keep up the old traditions of formal dress for formal occasions. Lochinvar's influence over the running of the castle was immense. Yet he was as unobtrusive as a good butler should be. You could forget he was there.

The Poet opened the front door. Squinting into the low sunlight, he looked towards a group of his older protegés kicking a ball. They were tall, at ease with themselves, with expanses of confident bare flesh despite the weak winter sun. There were eight of them, with some younger children nearby. Twenty-two altogether, with five adults to teach and three others to care for them. He had wanted more children. He wanted to build a community of strong and clear-thinking people, bringing them up away from the dangers and struggle of an underground life in the City.

The idea had first come to him when a plague outbreak underground had wiped out large numbers of Outsiders, leaving three orphan babies without anyone to care for them. He hadn't particularly liked babies, or even children, but as he had looked around the demoralised and weakened group which he was supposed to lead, he had seen the waste of it all. He imagined the lifeblood of the Outsiders, the people he loved, pouring away into nothing. So he had begun to construct his plan, sending messages through his contacts amongst the rural Outsiders, and had eventually been put in touch with Lochinvar, a man who clearly shared his vision from the start.

Within weeks, the Poet had arrived at the castle, with a few other adults following in secret and the orphan babies being brought one by one. But there were not enough babies. So, through Milton, he sent word to all the groups of Outsiders – any parents who wanted their babies to have a better life could hand them over and they would be brought up in safety. He told Milton to go to any lengths to find and save healthy babies.

Parents were not interested. They preferred to keep their babies with them. The Poet could not understand this. He had never had children. He was frustrated by what seemed to him like selfishness, a stubborn refusal to look further than their own feelings. But he should have realised that love is selfish – he had been in love himself, after all. Not so long before.

Then had come the baby whose grey eyes were deep as the sea as she stared at him. Her parents, so Milton had said, had been killed by the Pols and they had died bravely, loving their daughter, entrusting her to him. Looking into her silent eyes, the Poet felt something stir, and he vowed then that he would look after her, would love her on their behalf.

His plan was more ambitious now, developing from long conversations with Lochinvar. These children could one day change society. He was building a community which would eventually return to the City and overthrow the rotten system. He had no clear idea of how they might do that – it was impossible to know until the secrets of Center Tower were revealed. Lochinvar was convinced it could be done, that one day they would find a way. Meanwhile, the Poet could dream.

Were his dreams all going to be ruined now?

'Boys, girls. Over here now, please.' They stopped kicking the ball, though not immediately. A couple of seconds ignoring him, just enough but not too much, and then they lounged towards him as slowly as they reasonably could.

Livia and Marcus were in the lead. They walked shoulder to shoulder, easy together. Walking with sprung energy, as though they could start to run at any moment, they were both blond, the tips of their hair still sun-streaked from days spent outside during the long-gone summer. Though the weather had tanned Marcus' skin and Livia was naturally paler they could have been brother and sister. They had lived together all their lives as though they were. And yet they were not.

Tavius was behind them, on his own, darker haired, caramel skinned, thinner, gangly, but moving with long careless strides. Tavius was usually on his own. It was not that he was unpopular. Just that he seemed to surround himself with a barrier. 'Don't touch me,' it seemed to say. 'I don't need it.' The others followed straggling. The Poet watched them all as they approached. Annoyed as he might often be, exasperated by their casual ignorance and lack of care, yet deep down, if he ever thought about it, he loved and cared for them like a father.

Marcus smiled with an irritating arrogance as he approached, tossing a cricket ball from hand to hand. Marcus was never still, always fizzing with unnecessary energy. His thick hair was tangled as usual. He threw the ball to Livia and pulled an old jumper over his head, his muscles hard and weather-browned. All the young people were outside at every opportunity, playing football or working in the vegetable garden, or riding ponies or shooting rabbits, pheasants, deer even. Thanks to them, the kitchen was always full.

Tavius pulled a comb from his pocket and ran it once through his hair. Tavius always moved slowly, as though there was nothing to hurry for. As though the world must wait for him. And if it didn't, he wouldn't care.

Livia swung her slim hips as she walked, easy as a cat. She needed no make-up, so she put on too much on purpose. Her jaw was strong and prominent, even when she was not angry, her skin as smooth and round as opal. As she walked, she was tying her thick hair back loosely with what looked like a T-shirt. She let large strands escape and cover her eyes. The Poet itched to tell her to brush it, but he knew she would brush it and then tie it too loosely and the hair would fall out again as if it mocked him. Her eyes were the grey of a cold sea. As she came near, she fixed her gaze on a place above the Poet's head and smiled innocently.

'Yes?'

'Livia, I will not have you using that sort of language, if you don't mind. And Marcus—'

'What language? I am sorry, I don't remember . . .' she said, her round glossed lips pouting slightly.

'You know perfectly well what I mean, Livia. I am not deaf. Nor am I stupid. Nor am I entirely ignorant of the words you young people use. Now Marcus, what were you doing to Livia?'

'Doing to Livia? I would never do anything to Liv. Honest. Did I do anything to you, Liv?' He touched her on the arm, wide-eyed.

'Yes, well, never mind that now,' said the Poet, irritated again. He would get nowhere with this one. Besides, he knew that Livia could look after herself and that Marcus would not hurt her and, anyway, it was all a game. But now their games frustrated him. They would have to stop playing. They would have to grow up. Fast.

'Was there anything else?' asked Livia.

'Yes, all of you go to the classroom now, please. I have something to tell you.' His legs went weak at the thought and he felt a twinge in his knee. He passed a hand across his forehead, pressed his temple.

'Are you all right?' asked Marcus.

'Yes, I am perfectly all right, thank you, Marcus. I will see you inside.' He watched them go in. Young people without a care in their world.

2

The boys and girls dawdled towards the castle and into the huge panelled room which they used as a classroom. High-backed dining chairs sat untidily around an enormous old table.

'Wonder what this is about?' said Livia. Tavius shrugged. He pulled on a thick jumper, the milk-chocolate colour matching his skin, and sat down, rocking back in his chair. He picked up a book and started reading.

'God knows. Just PB getting het up about something, probably. We'll soon find out,' said Marcus as he took the football and bounced it on the floor. 'Come on, Liv, challenge you.'

'Can't be arsed.' And she sat on the table near Tavius while Marcus and the others fooled around with the ball. She looked at her fingernails. The black varnish was chipped. She would have to redo it – but she didn't have much left. 'I was hoping our visitor was Tarka. I need new stuff,' she complained. Tarka was their lifeline. She was a local country Outsider who had a way of obtaining clothes and make-up and luxuries from the traders at the edge of the City. At the castle, they paid her in vegetables or freshly-killed meat.

Madame Bovary relied on her too. And all the girls knew perfectly well that it was the dermoplactive cream that kept the teacher's forehead so artificially smooth. Not to mention the electrolon underwear they knew she wore.

'You always need new stuff,' said Tavius, scathingly. Still reading his book, he rolled an old cricket ball backwards and forwards along his arm and when it dropped he caught it before it reached the floor. He had hardly seemed to move and yet his long arm was there in time.

Livia said nothing. Something in the Poet's eyes, in the way he had looked, had disturbed her. The others never seemed to think much about the future, but Livia did. She thought about it now.

'Do you ever wonder what it's all for, Tav?' she asked.

He looked up, stared into the distance. 'Sure. Happiness. What everyone wants. Freedom. To do what you want.' He went back to his book, face blank.

'It's not *what* it's all for, it's *who* it's all for,' shouted Marcus, passing them with the ball. 'Or – sorry, Cicero – I should say "whom". Anyway, it's all for me, of course. I'm the Poet's natural heir.' And he whirled by, bouncing the ball with alternate hands.

'Shut it, big mouth,' said Tavius.

'But what are we here for?' repeated Livia.

58

'All part of the divine plan,' said Tavius, a cool sneer on his face.

'You don't believe that old stuff. All part of PB's plan, more like.'

'Yeah, well, no point in worrying about that now. We've got ages before we have to deal with that, whatever it is. I'm trying to read, Livia.'

Livia was silent. She picked up a book too. Ovid's poetry. Pretended to read it. She might seem to stride through life with careless confidence but she was frightened for the future. Frightened of what she would have to do. Or not *knowing* what she would have to do. The others seemed so unconcerned.

She had a recurring dream, which had only begun quite recently: in it, the earth beneath her feet was a thin skin and underneath was water. At any moment, if she put a step wrong, the skin would burst beneath her. Always in the dream, however carefully she trod, the skin eventually split and each time she would wake up, soaked in sweat, without ever knowing what it was she had done wrong.

Did this insecurity come from being an orphan? But the others were orphans too and it didn't seem to bother them. She had been told about her parents dying in the plague. But she wanted to know more. What had it been like to die underground, without medicine? To have no choices? How would her life have been different if she had not been an orphan?

The adults came into the classroom, looking solemn. Madame Bovary smiled at Livia and the others. Old people should look old, thought Livia. And that lipstick is too bright – looks as if her lips are bleeding into the cracks in her skin. A moment later the Poet came in. He seemed to be limping more than usual.

'Sit down, please.' He stood at the head of the table and held onto the edge. And spoke. They sat through it all in silence. The last ray of sunlight slipped past the window and the room became grey. Livia shivered.

Marcus spoke. His voice, normally so confident, sounded suddenly small. 'How will we get there?'

'Lochinvar will take you to the edge of the City – a day and a half, maybe two, in the cart. He will tell you where to meet Milton.'

'How will we communicate with you?' Tavius asked.

'Same way Milton does now. Through a computer belonging to one of the Specials – his daughter's friend.'

'What will we wear? I can't be seen dead in this old stuff in the City,' said Livia.

'We can go to the entertainment zones!' said Marcus.

'Will we get a solacar?' asked Livia.

'Don't be ridiculous. Of course, you will not. You are going to be Outsiders, not Citizens.'

Dr Grimm put his head in his hands. The other teachers looked at each other. How would these teenagers ever be able to change anything more complicated than their own hairstyles?

The Poet left Cicero to take charge. He caught Livia's attention. 'Livia, I need to speak to you. In my room.' She stood up. Arching her eyebrows at the others, she followed him along the corridor to his study. A fire burned in the hearth.

'Have a seat, Livia. Would you like something to drink?' He seemed nervous.

'No, thank you.' She sat down and watched him as he poured himself a drink. She wished he wouldn't wear that kilt all the time. And the thick jumper that still smelt of her childhood. Stories and poems read to her and the others by firelight with the snow falling silent outside. Or lying on their stomachs in the sweet warm summer grass as his voice sang the rhythms of the ancient words. She wished he would brush his hair. And wash it more often. And it was too long for someone of his age. She fiddled with a piece of her own hair. And waited.

'I want to tell you . . . about your parents.' Her heart stopped. Then started again, faster. 'You know they died just after you were born. You have always believed they died in the plague. The time has come for you to know the truth.' He paused. Took a deep breath. 'They died for you.' Livia did not want to hear this. Yet she didn't tell him to stop. Even though she could feel the pain before it came.

He continued. 'They gave you to us soon after you were born. But they were shot dead by the Pols. Milton told me. He saw it happen.'

Livia tried to take this in. 'How do you mean, they "gave me" to you?'

'They wanted you to have a better life. They wanted you to grow up here, be strong, be educated perfectly and to be free. To help change society. To . . .'

'They *gave me up* to change society? Oh, really? So, they loved me THAT much?' her sarcasm blazed through swimming eyes.

'Of course they loved you. They loved you more than anything, more than themselves. Their names were Ten and Merrilee. You have no idea what your life would have been like under the streets of the City, among the Outsiders, living like prisoners, powerless. They died to give you something different.'

'But I would have had my parents! I would have had my parents! Not you and Grimm and all the others who bore us to death with your latin verbs and ancient poems and pointless sodding pointless stories!' She stood up, her words shaking, her hands cold, and shouted, 'Why did you tell me this? I didn't want to know!'

'Because you need to know your story. Because they had great hopes for you. Because we all have great hopes for you. That was what they called you. Hope.'

'Hope! Hope? How bloody corny! How king bloody corny can you get? Didn't they have more imagination than that?'

'No, actually they didn't, Livia. And mind your language, please. They were Specials. You know what Specials are. They couldn't fully use their imagination.' Yes, she knew. So, not even real Outsiders?

He continued. 'They wanted you to grow up free of that, to grow your brain and have everything they couldn't have. Real choice, real free will, real understanding. Freedom, Livia!'

Freedom! Was this what freedom felt like? Her chest was pounding. 'May I go now?' She stood up, straight, her eyes glistening, her cheeks flushed. Her jaw was clenched so tightly that her neck hurt.

The Poet stood between her and the door. She walked as firmly as she could towards it, not meeting his eyes. He took her by the shoulders but she stood hard and cold. 'Livia, I trust you. Your parents loved you and I love you for them. They died because they loved you. What greater sacrifice could there be?' He moved slightly, perhaps to kiss her forehead, but she didn't move, just felt trapped inside. And he stopped. For a tiny moment she wanted to be held. She wanted it almost more than anything. But she couldn't bring herself to let him. He dropped his hands and she walked out of the door.

Suddenly she turned back towards him. 'What about the others? What about their parents?'

'They died from plague. Just as you were all told before. You were different. Given by your parents to be special.'

As Livia walked down the corridor, she could barely breathe. So, she was the only one whose parents had given her away? She felt something inside swell and choke her. Tears started from her eyes. She forced them back, hardened her heart till nothing could get out, held her breath till the tears disappeared. How could the Poet have lied to her? How could her parents have loved her? She would never believe it. She spat inside with anger.

Livia did not return to the classroom. Instead she ran up the stairs, across a landing, through a door and up some more stairs. To the room where her bed was. From under the bed she pulled her ancient guitar. She forced a chair under the door handle.

She smashed her fingers across the strings and shouted

aloud at the spearing pain. Again, and again. It was the sort of pain you need not mind about. The sort of pain that helped shut out the rest. Then she hardened her jaw, closed her eyes and disappeared down inside herself.

This is how I will deal with it.

I am only crying now to wash it out of me. I don't see why I can't cry when I've just discovered my parents gave me away to save the world. Though personally I think it would make more sense to laugh! I mean, what planet did they think they were on? Good thing they're dead if you ask me.

I am going back to the others now. As soon as my eyes have stopped being red. I'll put some more make-up on. Maybe in the City I'll be able to get better stuff, too. God, I look awful. Fatty eyes.

Why the hell did this have to happen to me? Who needs parents? If they'd only waited around long enough to ask me, I'd have told them I'd rather be a Citizen. Why did my flaming parents have to think they were so special?

Right, I'm going down now and no one is going to know about this. No one is ever, ever, EVER going to know that my parents gave me away.

Livia put her guitar gently back under the bed and went downstairs, biting the side of her lip. She held her head high, her jaw firm. The centres of her eyes glistened like deep water in the night.

Three days later, and the early morning hung dark and wet. Icy rain sliced down the windowpanes and wind rattled the glass. The trees in the distance were charcoal shadows.

They all stood awkwardly in the hall, waiting for Lochinvar to bring the cart to the door. Ordinary chat seemed pointless now, and all the important things had been said. The last days had been spent in a whirl of instructions. The Poet and the other teachers had tried to prepare them for their uncertain mission. Whether any of them fully understood the dangers or importance was another matter. The teachers doubted it.

Lochinvar had prepared something for them. A small bottle each. It contained, he explained, strong oil of lemon, tea-tree and orange. A couple of drops, inhaled or rubbed into each nostril every now and then, would ward off any virus, he assured them. Breathe through your nose, he said. He seemed excited, positive, not doubtful like the teachers.

The three who were going and their friends who were staying had all laughed and teased each other, spending time in foolish games, as though all this meant nothing. The Poet's spirits sank.

He had watched Livia since telling her about her parents. She seemed unaffected. He had taken a risk in suddenly telling her the truth. The risk was that she would go to pieces. But what he hoped was that instead she would be inspired to fight. That the fire in her would burn. But playing with fire was dangerous, he knew. And now she simply seemed her usual careless self. Perhaps he had misjudged her spirit. He needed that spirit.

There was something special about her. He had known it that first day he saw her. Most babies have blue eyes but hers were grey even then. Something in those grey eyes reminded him of himself. Something determined.

A scrunch on the gravel outside. Everyone turned to the door.

'Your carriage awaits,' said Stevenson. He opened the door and in the sheeting dawn rain stood the cart, drawn by two ponies, driven by Lochinvar. There was a flimsy-looking cover over the back, a waterproof sheet tied down to poles at each corner. The sides flapped and tugged in the wind.

'Right, everyone. No point in hanging around,' said the Poet. Marcus was the first to walk up to the teachers and hold out his hand. Livia envied the way he could switch to being so convincingly adult. The others followed and there was a minute of hugging and handshaking and slapping of backs. Even Dr Grimm managed to find some words of encouragement.

Livia hugged her other friends tightly. She could see Marcus doing the same. Tavius, as always, was more reserved, but even he shook hands as he said goodbye to everyone. There was no laughter now, just tight lips and white faces.

Livia came to the Poet last. Her emotions were so mixed that she didn't know what to say. This was the man who had brought her up. And this was the man who had deceived her. Who had set her a task that she did not want to do.

He had said he trusted her. But what did that mean? How did you know whether adults meant what they said when so much of it was calculated to make you into something? Something *they* wanted you to be. They talked about choices and how education would give endless strength. But now, what choice was she being given?

The Poet took her by the shoulders and pulled her to him. She said nothing and a moment later she moved away, though not roughly. She looked at him but his grey eyes made her uncomfortable, as though she was looking inside herself, and she glanced away. 'I trust you, Livia. I know you can do it,' he said.

Just the sort of thing adults always say when they want you to try hard. For effect again? Did he really trust her? Or was it just words?

How could he let her go? On a mission that he admitted was dangerous? How could her parents have let her go? What did love mean if that was what it did?

She mumbled something, turned away. Almost turned back again and hugged him. Almost.

3

They picked up their bags, swung them over their shoulders, and pulled their collars up to cover their ears. A moment later they were clambering into the cart, the rain sliding down their faces. As it rattled and lurched away, they waved at the figures standing on the steps of Balmoral Castle, its crumbling battlements silhouetted against the moleskin sky. Livia had a strange and fleeting feeling of pity for the Poet, standing there with his grey hair whipped aside in the wind. He looked surprisingly and suddenly powerless, as though he too was being swept along by something outside his control.

So? It was his decision. We could have all stayed together. Gone somewhere else. But no — he always has to know best. Serves him right.

They sat without speaking as the cart clattered across the terrace and down the potholed avenue towards the road. The rain spattered the plastic sheet and the wind flicked their hair in their eyes and chilled their skin. Marcus pulled the flap down so that the worst of the wind was kept outside and with frozen hands tied it in place. They all sat close together, the warmth of their breath mixing in the cold morning air.

After a while, the rocking of the cart lulled Livia and she closed her eyes. She could hear the others talking, but she was not in the mood. 'Liv? Liv?' She felt someone shake her. It was Marcus.

'Everything OK? You're quiet.'

'Fine,' she said. But her eyes stung and she knew if she said anything more she would let go. She pulled her scarf up so her face was covered and Marcus left her alone.

She found herself drumming her fingers hard against the wood of the cart. She wished she had her guitar. The others had raised their eyebrows when she said she was going to bring it. 'What's it to you? I'll be the one carrying it,' she had snapped.

'It'll get in the way, Liv,' someone had said.

'Don't you think you've got enough to worry about without hauling that guitar everywhere?' said someone else.

'Yeah, well you won't be with me, will you?'

'It'll hold us up,' said Tavius.

'No it won't,' interrupted Marcus. 'Liv won't let it, will you, Liv?'

'Whadever,' muttered Livia. Why couldn't they just look after themselves and let her make her choices?

She didn't take it in the end. Inside herself, she knew it would be in the way and she didn't want anyone saying, 'I told you so.' Besides, not taking it gave her even more reason to be angry.

She shut her eyes and drummed the beat with her fingers against the wooden floor until her hands hurt.

I should have looked him in the eye. I should have said something. Because now he's going to think . . . So? I don't care, do I? He doesn't, even though he always says he does, so why should I? All this love crap. Like when I was small and I'd get a punishment and it was always, 'It's only because we love you.' Crap. It's because they want you to be good. They want to make you into something, mould you. But I'm not putty.

And my parents. So, they gave me away because they loved me? How does that work exactly? If I had something I loved, I'd keep it.

I was OK till he told me that. I was just me and now I'm partly me and partly someone else too. Like, you think your life would just change gradually so you wouldn't notice. A little bit at a time. Well, it's not true. There are massive holes you fall in. Ocean deep. Mountain high.

Makes me think of that story Cicero told us. A thought experiment, he called it.

Imagine a man, he said. Odysseus it was in the

imagining, but it could be anyone. He's on long journey, on his ship. And a part of the ship breaks, so he chucks the broken bit of wood overboard and replaces it with a new bit of wood. I don't know, maybe he stopped at an island to get the wood. Anyway, a bit further on another bit of the ship is broken so he replaces that with a new bit of wood. It's still Odysseus' ship, of course. And this continues, until by the time he reaches his destination, every single bit of the ship has been replaced by new wood.

The question is, said Cicero, is it still Odysseus' ship? And if not, when exactly did it become not Odysseus' ship? Because no part of it is the ship he started out in.

Of course, if Odysseus had just scrapped the whole ship in one go and bought another one, it'd be easy. The original ship would be dead and gone and the new one would be obviously a different ship. But the fact that it was gradual changes everything.

Well, it's the same with people. Am I the same person as I was a year ago, just with some new bits, or has so much of me changed that I am dead and gone and have been replaced by someone totally different? And when did I become not me?

Does everybody think like this? I bet Marcus and Tavius don't.

I wish this journey was over. I'm cold and wet and hungry and everyone keeps sniffing. I've got cramp and I'm bored.

Wonder what the place is like where we're staying tonight. Lochinvar only said, 'Don't expect too much.' So it's not a castle then, or if it is it'll be ruined. Like most of the rest of this country.

It'll be different in the City. It can't be as bad as they say. At least there's no weather. Except when it's scheduled. What a brilliant system!

I'm glad I'm with Marcus. Even Tavius, too. I used to feel sorry for Tavius when we were small. He was always on the outside of every game. You'd ask him in, eventually, because you'd feel guilty, but then you'd wish you hadn't. Because he didn't know how to join in and he made you feel uncomfortable. He'd stand there with his big brown eyes and say, 'But why do you have to do that?' or 'You didn't tell me that rule.' But now he's built this shell and he looks OK inside his shell. He doesn't really DO friends. Which makes it easier somehow. You don't have to try. You can't fall out with someone who doesn't care enough to get angry.

And Marcus. He's not afraid of anything. Like, if there was a crisis, you'd want Marcus there. He makes everything seem easy.

But he has never had to do something like this. None of us has.

What's going to happen?

And why does it have to be us?

After a few hours they came to a halt. Climbed stiffly out of the cart and stretched their legs. The rain had stopped and the sky was a clear pearl blue, though the breeze was still mint-cold. The northern midday sun sat low above the hills. An eagle swung overhead before flying off into the distance.

Lochinvar came round to them, a drip wobbling from the end of his nose. 'I'm changing the ponies. Farm just round the corner. Stay here.' And he unhitched the ponies and disappeared, his walnut-brown bow-legs striding between the two tired animals. This was the system when travelling in the country. Solacars only worked in the City and no Citizen ever dreamt of coming to the cold and unregulated countryside, so transport was only by primitive cart. The rural Outsiders had evolved a system of borrowing and hiring ponies and, as long as you came back the same way, you always ended up with your own pony back again.

On the next stage of the journey, their spirits were higher. Freedom seemed like something they could almost grasp. They talked and laughed, even Tavius joining in sometimes. They imitated the teachers and invented absurd and exaggerated lives for them, usually involving sex.

They made up tunes to the words of all the poems they could remember. And when they couldn't remember any more, Tavius took out a tin whistle and played sad flutey songs that reminded them of mist and the sea and ancient stories of romance and tragedy. And as twilight thickened into darkness and it began to rain again, they were silent once more, pressed together, rocked by the movement of the cart.

A bond began to grow, different from the unthinking one that came from a lifetime together. They knew they had been chosen, that they were special. They began to feel each other's presence, to tune in, to need each other.

At last, they came to the place where they were staying the night. As they stepped from the cart, they looked around slowly. It was like something from a historical film. Seventeenth century maybe. The ground under their feet was churned with mud. Two small children stood staring at them, maybe two and five years old, their feet bare, their clothes filthy, their hair ragged. Pieces of broken wood and metal lay against the walls of the house, the wheel of a tractor here, a useless ladder there. Half the house was ruined, without a roof, ancient stonework crumbled by the centuries. The other half had a mixture of planks and sticks over the windows. A thin cat sat and watched slit-eyed from a ledge.

A woman appeared at the door. She was dressed in shapeless ancient trousers and a thick hand-knitted jumper. Her dusty hair lay limply around her shoulders.

She smiled her welcome with lips that were slate-thin and cracked. 'Lochinvar! We were so pleased to get your message. All of you, come in.' Her skin was red with broken veins and her cheekbones stuck out like a scrawny cat's shoulders.

They followed Lochinvar through the door. The woman shut it after them, with difficulty as it hung from one hinge. Inside was dark, the air heavy with wood-smoke. A fire burnt in the hearth. Livia's eyes stung. But at least it was warm.

'Sit down, all of you. I'll make some tea.' She managed to make tea and prepare slices of heavy bread and watery jam, at the same time as bathing the children in a tub before the fire. There was no running water, as far as they could see. The woman had heated it in a huge pan over the fire. 'I am sorry about this,' she smiled. 'This is the only room warm enough.'

They felt silenced by this poverty. They had never been outside Balmoral, where they had had free run of countless rooms, and where lemons grew in a hothouse and raspberries on canes in the summer; where there was solar-powered electricity to heat the water and power the washing machine and countless gadgets that they had taken for granted. They had not realised what they had. They were embarrassed to be eating the food at this woman's table while she never stopped working.

Even her hair was tired. Greasy like damp ashes.

If this was how Outsiders lived in the country, what was it like in the City, living underground? They began to realise the vastness of their task.

There was a noise outside. A shout, a man's voice, harsh. The woman stood up. 'My husband,' she said. The door scraped open and in came a wild-eyed man. He frowned when he saw the visitors. 'So, they're here,' he said to his wife. 'Haven't eaten all the food, have they?'

'No, dear, of course not,' she said, apologising with her eyes to Lochinvar and the others.

'Good evening, sir,' said Marcus. The others mumbled the same.

The man said nothing, only grunted, and went over to the tub where the children had been bathed. He started to remove his jacket, and his wife went to help him. That was when Livia saw it. The others noticed at the same time. Her stomach turned. The food rose in her throat and she couldn't help her fingers flying to her mouth. But she quickly took her hand away again in shame and pretended to scratch her face.

The man had an arm missing. But it was not that the arm was missing, it was what the stump looked like. Twisted and red, snarling and angry. The man didn't seem to notice or care as he used his other hand to scoop water over his face. His wife held out a towel for him to dry himself. With difficulty, he pulled on a clean shirt. And went up the stairs without a word.

'What happened, Ellen?' asked Lochinvar. 'That's recent.'

'Broke his arm,' she said. 'Bones sticking out through the flesh – compound fracture. It became infected.'

'Who did you find to amputate it?'

'I did it. Who else? He'd have died if I hadn't. I know people with the skills, but no one I could get in time.'

'It's changed him. He was never one for the chatter, but now . . .'

'He's given up. Used to be angry. Now he just doesn't care any more. What's the point, he says? He sometimes says we'd all be better off dead.'

She wiped her face with the back of her hand, and poured another cup of tea from a teapot with half a spout.

Livia and the others listened to all this in silence. They had nothing to say.

After the guests had eaten, the two small children came and sat shyly by the fire with them. The woman took out a battered book and read them stories, though she seemed to know them by heart. Livia sat hugging her knees, resting her chin on them, her mind drowsy with exhaustion and the heat from the fire on her face. These stories were the sounds of her childhood. She wished she could be a child again. With so much time left.

Soon the younger child was asleep, but the older one listened and listened, his cheeks becoming cherry-hot in the fire. And when the woman's eyes were red-rimmed with tiredness she scooped up the little one. 'Time for bed, sleepy heads,' she said to her children. Then, to her guests, 'I'll show you where you will all sleep. It's just a floor, I'm afraid.' They followed her up the stairs and through a leaning door. As they stared at the room, its rafters bare, a bucket catching rain in the corner, the woman turned to Livia. 'You look exhausted, love,' she said.

Don't call me love. You don't know me. Don't mess around with words.

'Yeah,' she replied. 'Suppose. Where's the bathroom?'

'You have a choice,' said the woman, smiling directly at her. 'There's a bucket on the landing. Or there's outside.' And that was a choice? 'And for washing, there's a bowl of water here.'

For a moment Livia just stood, not knowing where to turn. Then she chose. That's what you do when you have no choice. You make a choice. 'Outside,' she said.

'Come with me.' Leaving the small children, the woman led her down the stairs again, into the room where the man now sat staring with dull eyes into the fire. She took a thick stick from a pile, dipped it in a bucket of something, and held it in the fire, where it burst into flames. Handing it to Livia, she said, 'Follow me.' And she led her out into the wind, where the torch spluttered and struggled. Flames seemed to dive from it into the surrounding air. Livia held it as far from her as she could. The woman took her to a lean-to shed and showed her a hole where she could stick the torch. 'I can find my own way back,' said the woman as she left. 'And I'm sorry it's not what you are used to.' She said it without embarrassment.

'No. It's . . . it's fine.' Livia tried to speak politely but she knew her voice sounded false. When the woman had gone, she looked around her into the flickering gloom. Rotten wood, mildewed walls, an earth floor, a bucket with a hole in the bottom, over a pit in the ground. The sodden air stinking. A pile of dried grass and leaves beside the bucket. With horror, she guessed what they were for.

And spiders. Good thing she wasn't afraid of spiders. Just then, just as she was about to place the torch in its hole, something scuttled across the floor. Over her foot. She screamed. A cockroach, brown and shiny in the firelight. And another. She leapt backwards through the doorway, hit her head on the doorframe, and dropped the torch. It sizzled in a pool of water on the floor and, before she could pick it up, went out. She was in complete darkness. The rain lashed into the back of her head, plastering her hair to her neck.

For a moment, she stood there, her thoughts frozen. What could she do? She couldn't go back into the shed – it was pitch-black. There was only one alternative. The bucket on the landing. She turned and hurried with her head down through the slicing rain towards the house, where she could see a dim glow around the edges of the window shutters. Mud splattered as she ran. She felt like shouting at the wind, screaming her fury as wet hair whipped and flicked against her eyes and the rain flung itself at her face.

She could not wait to get to the City. The place where even the sun was regulated, obeying the Government's orders, and where it only rained at night. On the first three nights of the month. Anything would be better than this savage existence.

The woman looked up as Livia forced open the rickety door. She was sitting with Lochinvar, sharing a glass of something whisky-coloured. Her husband sat silently with his eyes closed.

'Something wrong, love?' she asked.

'I just . . . I just dropped the torch.' She knew she must look horrendous. She wanted to get away from them, not have them staring at her.

'Never mind, dear. Let's get you fixed with a fresh one, shall we? My and don't you look like a drowned rat? Poor love.'

'It doesn't matter,' muttered Livia, feeling herself go red. 'Really, I . . .'

'Oh well, if you're sure. But remember there's the bucket on the landing.'

How could I forget? And why does the woman have to go ON? Can't she just shut up and leave me alone and pretend I'm not here?

Later, Livia lay awake in her sleeping bag. The wooden floor was hard under her back. She heard the soft breathing of the others and wondered what they dreamt of. Were all their thoughts and dreams as complicated as hers?

'Liv?' It was Marcus, still awake too. 'Are you sure you're all right?' His voice so reasonable, so strong, so ignorant.

Don't ask. Don't ask. Don't bloody well ask, or you might not like the answer. I feel like a speck of dust floating on the

*skin of the water. What will happen when the wind blows hard
and the water shakes its skin away?*

'I'm fine.' And with her eyes closed, she squeezed her
thumbnail into the soft part of her finger until the pain
flooded through her and clutched at her heartbeat and
then washed away. There was a shuffling as Marcus
moved closer to her. His breath was warm on her ear.

'Don't worry about everything. We can do it – we
can do anything, remember? Besides, you're with me!
How can we fail?'

'Cocky sod,' she whispered back in the darkness.

'Seriously, Liv. It'll be fine. They wouldn't have sent
us if they hadn't believed in us. And if we don't manage
it, this Center Tower thing – so? We'll have tried.
That's all that matters. And then we can go back home
and . . . I don't know – you worry too much, that's all.
We'll be fine.'

'Yeah, I know,' she lied. And she found his hand and
squeezed it.

*But you haven't got someone who died so that you could do
this, have you? And that's what makes it different. You don't
have that anger. And guilt.*

*Something that happened to me before I can remember is
changing the way I am now. I am controlled by my past.*

'Goodnight, Marcus.' And he squeezed her hand in reply and left his fingers in hers. She felt the strength of his bones, the smallness of her hand in his. Later, when his fingers softened and she knew he was asleep, she slid her hand away from him. As her arm moved across the floor, her wrist brushed against a sharp splinter of wood. She pressed her flesh down hard, until the skin was pierced with a silent sort of popping sound. The pain sent a rush of something through her chest and she gasped. It was as though everything in her went with it, and out through the hole in her wrist.

I just love the way it hurts. Love the emotion and the realness. Love the way it mixes and churns you till you don't know what to think. Just feel.

You have to feel to live.

4

The next morning they were woken before it was light. Their joints were stiff with cold and the hardness of the floor. They had to break the ice on the water in the jug and they gasped with shock as they washed their faces.

Later, on the cart, their stomachs full from the bread and eggs that the woman could ill afford, they started the next stage of the journey in silence. As the City grew closer, they became less sure what to expect.

Up to now, the countryside had been wild and familiar. The hillsides had been strewn sometimes with heather and rocks, sometimes with black forests. Boulders and rusted metal from ancient wrecked cars lay alongside the road, and every now and then they had passed through ruined villages. Sometimes, branches had fallen across the road and they had had to stop to haul them aside. Dead bracken swayed in the wind. They had passed virtually no people. A man pushing turnips on a barrow, another herding a handful of sheep, a woman pulling two cows, their udders swaying between their bony legs. The people had looked at the cart with blank expressions, too exhausted by the struggle for food to wonder why they passed that way.

Towards the City. The Northern Zone cut a swathe down the west of the country, from where Glasgow had been down to what used to be Manchester. This Northern Zone, they knew, melded seamlessly into the Center Zone, which extended down as far as the area which used to be called London. To the east, and over much of the far west of the country, old Wales and the south west, most of what had been land was now under water, flood plain, carefully managed and dammed and desalinated, providing all the water the country needed. A few hills rose from the vast lake, many with the ruined spires of churches or the crumpled battlements of ancient walls. Under all these flood plains, they had been taught, lay countless towns, no longer needed now that Citizens all lived in the safety of the City. Altogether, the City was one sprawling mass, its climate controlled by the electroshield surrounding it. This electroshield had been created to detect and prevent the entry of the old terrorists, with their bombs and germs and chemicals. Now, however, terror had given up. There was nothing for its hatred to feed on. Everyone was too content.

Gradually, now, they noticed signs of a different environment. On a hill in the distance glinted the huge reflective solar panels, producing power for the City. In another direction stretched endless armies of shining windmills. The City would never run short of energy. This was fortunate, since the world's oil supply had dried up long ago. And in the farthest distance, if they squinted, they could just see the silver spaghetti streaks of a moontrain line. These were the high-speed tubes which surrounded the outsides of the City. Inside each, a solar-powered train – one for each tube – shot at enormous speeds to its destination. It was possible to go from one end of the City to the other, snaking along the edge for more than 700 kilometres, in less than two hours. And all without seeing anything of what was outside. The Citizens would not want to see. They had everything they needed in the sterile safety of inside.

After a while, the travellers found themselves approaching one of these silver tubes. Livia, Marcus and Tavius looked at each other nervously and shivered as they passed right underneath it. Its slim cigar-shape soared above them, 40 metres high, supported every kilometre or so by the thinnest struts, like spider silk in the distance. Perhaps this one was taking passengers to one of the virt-reality holiday resorts. Perhaps the Safari or the Tropical Rainforest. What would it be like? To experience a rainforest without going there, to see a snake three inches from your face but not need to fear it?

'Wow!' said Tavius, driven from his usual languidness by the sight. 'Would I love to go on that! I'd pick the virt-moon. I've always wanted to do that moon walk thing!'

'Nah, it's the Arctic-Trek one for me. I fancy myself as the "I may be some time" guy. The hero.'

'The one who dies, you mean? Frostbite would suit you,' said Livia. 'I'd do the Rock Chick Experience, me. Me and my guitar.' Except, of course, that the guitar wasn't with her. Underneath the bravado, she felt cold and afraid. Now that the City was close, she couldn't shake off the shadow of it. Until now, it had seemed far enough away not to fear.

Around a corner, the cart creaked to a halt. Lochinvar's face appeared in the opening. 'Right, time to move. And quick. We are in sight of the City.' He could hardly look at them. There was too much at stake. Lochinvar knew the risks. He had known these three since they were babies. Had seen them all arrive, pink-cheeked and yelling, in the arms of Milton. His whole task since then had been to keep them safe, to acquire what they needed, to help them grow into their destiny. Everything rested on their success now.

He tied the ponies to a tree. 'Follow me,' he said. Livia's heart lurched. This was the beginning. The beginning of the rest of her life. Nothing would ever be the same again. And for a moment, just briefly, she reached out with strange excitement towards the future.

They stumbled down the slope of a hill and onto a cracked road, its surface blistered and peeling from years of weather. Now, grass grew from the crevices in the swollen tarmac and scraggy heather sprang from the dry surface. The wind whipped dust into their eyes and they sensed the end of something, too. The last flurry before the City took control. Nature's final spit.

Lochinvar took them off the track. A thicket of scrawny shrubs lay before them. 'In here,' he said, and began to push his way in. They followed, their line broken now. Livia went first, her hair torn by thorns as she held branches aside for the others to pass by.

And suddenly, there it was. A huge hole in the side of a hill. Black, deep, endless. They looked at each other.

'Here you are,' said Lochinvar. 'It takes you right into the City, through the tunnels where the underground trains used to go. You walk to the first junction, and then you'll be met by Milton. It'll take you about half an hour, maybe more. If he's not there, wait for him. It will be dark – stick to the left wall of the tunnel.' He paused, looked awkward. 'Well, I'd better be going.' He wiped his hands on his shorts. Held out a hand to Marcus and Tavius. He held out a hand to Livia, but instead of taking it she flung her arms around him. He smelt of tobacco and peat and gunpowder and books with pages brindled by age. He smelt of home.

'Take care, now,' he said with a voice cracked with unusual fervour. 'We are relying on you. I know you can do it.' And somehow, when Lochinvar said it, Livia could believe him. His eyes burned with something like passion.

Unable to speak, the three of them looked one more time at the daylight, the fresh air and the distant hills, and walked firmly into the tunnel. The darkness swallowed them up and Lochinvar stayed for a while before heading home.

They had looked small as they went into the darkness. Too young. He knew their faults and strengths. He understood the gaps between the words they said. Take Marcus, his cocky swagger, his refusal to admit fear – Lochinvar could see through it and he worried how Marcus would react when real danger came. And as for Tavius, everyone thought he cared about nothing, but Lochinvar had seen him as a younger child gazing after other children playing together and had watched his face harden as he was left out of their games. He had seen that hardness turn to a cool shell, a casual smile, a refusal to become too close to anyone.

And Livia. He saw how she appeared so spiky, earthquake angry, how unpredictable she was. There was something hurting inside her. Look at her when she played her guitar. He had never liked its twangy sound but he could see how her whole body wrapped around it when she played. He had helped her replace the strings with ancient piano wire when they snapped. And he was the one who had found it in the attic three years before. He remembered how her eyes had lit up when she saw it and how she had strummed till her fingers were red and sore.

Yes, he cared about them, more than they realised. They would probably never know just how much he wanted them to succeed, he thought. They probably saw him as simply the caretaker of the castle, nothing more important. They probably laughed behind his back when he told again the stories of his ancestors, the proud butlers to the royal family.

One day, they would know better. One day, they would understand his role in their lives. Meanwhile, he could be patient as he waited and prayed for their successful and safe return.

Part Three

Going Underground

They cannot scare me with their empty spaces
Between the stars — on stars where no human race is.
I have it in me so much nearer home
To scare myself with my own desert places.

Desert Places by Robert Frost

1

They didn't speak as they moved away from the light. As the darkness closed in further, thick and damp, the only sounds were the wet crunch of footsteps and the rasp of breathing. And, when they listened carefully, the steady drip of water. They strained their ears for other sounds. What creatures could live in these tunnels?

Several times, Livia thought she heard a scuttling. The flesh on her neck crawled and her breathing became faster. She tried to slow her heartbeat. She found herself walking with her fingers spread wide as though she was expecting something to leap at her.

They walked in single file, keeping close to the wall, slowly, unable to see the ground beneath their feet clearly. Tavius walked in front, Livia in the middle, Marcus behind. Livia was glad she was in the middle.

The atmosphere was wet and old, thick with moisture

and decay and airlessness. It was the tangy smell of rusted metal and mildewed earth and insects that hide and die under stones.

Soon the light from the end of the tunnel had almost completely disappeared and they could sense only the hard shape of the wall at their left shoulders. The blackness fell like cloth around their heads, heavy, as if it wanted to stop them breathing.

Seconds, minutes, uncountable, passed. Time twisted and ground to a halt. It was as though they were in a place that was nowhere.

Still none of them had spoken. They were all lost in their own thoughts, trying to control their own fears. Despite the cold clammy air, Livia was beginning to sweat under the weight of her backpack and the layers of clothes.

Tavius stumbled, almost fell. He swore.

'You OK?' asked Livia, her voice loud in the blackness.

'Yeah, keep going,' he muttered.

'No, wait. Let's stop a minute,' said Marcus. 'I need some water.' And he fumbled to get his water bottle from the side of his backpack. They stood close together, their breath mixing in the cold air.

It was then, just as they each wondered whether to voice the fear that threatened to overpower them, that they heard it. A scuttling. A padding. Scratching on the old metal train tracks.

They moved closer to each other. Livia gripped an arm – Tavius or Marcus, she couldn't tell. She could hear the blood in her ears, feel her heart crashing in her chest. She tried to breathe quietly, slowly, to make herself undetectable to whatever it was in the tunnel.

Into the frozen moment came Tavius' voice, thin and strained. 'Over there,' he whispered. 'Over there.' The others peered around, trying to see which direction he meant. Marcus breathed, a long-drawn out word that seemed to merge with the dripping walls, 'Jeees-us.'

'What the hell is it?' whispered Livia.

Eyes. Yellow pinpoints. Impossible to tell how far away. Low down, unmoving.

'Don't move,' said Livia.

She looked a little to the right. Was that more eyes? How many? And a shuffling sound. Whatever creatures these were, they were coming closer.

'Show them we're not afraid,' said Tavius, firmly. 'Move forward. Now.'

Together they took one step forward. And another. A snarling sound snaked its way towards them. They stopped. The eyes moved closer.

'Bad idea,' said Marcus. 'Shit. What now?' His voice was shaking.

Livia's foot brushed against a stone. She stooped and picked it up, felt its coldness in her hand. And threw it as hard as she could at the eyes. There was a yelp and a furious snarling. A rushing, scampering, scratchy sound of claws and scattering stones. And the eyes had gone.

'I was just about to do that,' said Marcus.

'Yeah, right,' said Livia. She felt a new power, just beginning. 'We should all carry stones,' she said. And they scrabbled around for what they could find. Marcus found a piece of metal with a jagged edge and carried it in front of him like a sword, a stone in his other hand. They walked on, watching for the eyes.

Every now and then the darkness was lightened by holes in the roof, gratings through which grey daylight speared. But soon they found themselves going downhill more steeply, and the holes became fewer, more distant. In this darkness, they would never know when they had come to the junction, thought Livia. How long had they been walking? Half an hour? Less?

Peering through the black, she thought she could see a tiny light ahead. At first she thought it was the eyes again, but gradually she could see that it was just one light, a pinprick, but growing larger.

'Look!' she whispered urgently.

'Yeah, I know. I've been watching it,' replied Marcus. The light went off. A few moments later it went on again. As they walked towards it, they could see that it was shining straight at them, almost unmoving. Now it was lighting their faces. They looked at each other? Milton? There was only one thing to do: they walked forward towards the light.

The light did not waver. They walked on, every sense alert. Every muscle ready. Together in a line now, not single file. Shoulders almost touching. Livia's hands were sweating.

The light shone straight in their eyes. They could just make out the shape of a figure standing behind it, tall and slim. As they approached, they could see that it was a girl, of a similar age to them, with thick hair plaited and hanging over one shoulder. She didn't smile at them.

'Your names?'

'I'm Marcus, this is Livia and he's Tavius.' The three of them said hello, held out their hands.

The girl didn't move. 'Pleased to meet you,' she said, her voice as bland as milk.

'Where's Milton?' asked Livia, suspicious. 'We were told he would meet us.'

'He's ill. You've got me instead. Let's go.'

'How far do we have to go?' asked Marcus, politely, as the girl turned away.

'Far enough.' She began to walk away quickly. The

boys followed but Livia stopped to adjust her sock which had slipped down inside her shoe.

'Just a minute!' she called, irritated.

The girl turned and shone the torch at her. 'Hurry up! The dogs avoid the torch but you have to stay close.'

Dogs! That was all it was! Livia stood up, although her sock was still uncomfortable.

'And don't imagine they're tame,' the girl continued as though she had read their minds. 'They're feral. They hunt in packs and they're always hungry. We lost a child last month. Also, depends what type they are. There's a pack near here that's a mixture of rottweiler and bull mastiff.' She said it with relish.

As they tried to match the girl's fast pace, their breathing quickened and Livia felt herself sweat. The girl did not seem out of breath at all. Livia's shoe was now rubbing against her heel and every step became more painful. She wanted to stop, but she couldn't have asked again. Not with the girl driving ahead like this. The two boys were moving fast, too, and Livia felt herself beginning to be left behind. She quickened, trying to ignore the pain. And the feeling of eyes watching her back.

Round a corner, she became aware of another sound. A rushing noise, and cold air on her face. A different smell. Fish. Dead water. Something rotten. The girl held up her hand and stopped. 'Stay here,' she ordered. She moved ahead, lithe and silent as a panther, and peered around a corner. She whistled, loud and long. And again. They waited. Livia strained to hear anything. The girl clearly was not going to explain. Within a minute, they could hear a low whirring sound and she gestured for them to follow her.

When they rounded the corner, they could see a narrow channel of black water. A solaboat pulled to a halt and rocked on the canal in front of them. They had seen these things on the digi. Shaped like a torpedo, completely enclosed, sleek and smooth, black. The lid was pushed back and a man gestured for them to climb in. He barely looked at them as he helped them into the boat. They sat on the strangely soft seats and, when the girl put on her harness, they copied her. The man closed the lid and the boat moved off, slowly at first until it left the narrow channel and they could see that they were on a vast slice of water. Through the smoked windows they could make out the tall stretched buildings to each side, the snaking silver tubes for solatrains and, far in the high distance, the metallic cloudless sky, violet through the tinted glass. They were in the City.

'Is this the central canal?' asked Marcus, trying to make conversation with the girl. Leave her alone, thought Livia. She deserves no better.

'Yes,' said the girl. Then, after a pause, 'This is a waterkab. Hold tight. It's fast.' Suddenly, the solaboat shot away at high speed, almost lifting out of the water. They were pushed back against their seats by the force. Livia gasped. Marcus and Tavius gripped their armrests and grinned, their eyes wide. The girl ignored them all.

Music, tinny and distant, was piped through the boat. Livia recognised the tune. *Greensleeves*. But she couldn't identify the instruments playing it. It was jangly, wiry. It was tepid. It wasn't like the real music they were used to at Balmoral, with shape and form and passion and temperature. The girl leant forward and tapped on the dark smoked panel behind the boatman. The man's voice came through an intercom, 'Sorry. Forgot. You don' like it. Whadever.' The noise stopped and there was only the rhythmic crash of boat on water.

The girl stared straight ahead. Livia tried to look at her without seeming to. She wore a grey coat, cord, tailored, tied at her tiny waist by a belt. Skin-tight slicks beneath it, bare ankles and shoes moulded to her little feet. Her black hair was thick and very long, the plait almost to her waist. She wore no make-up and yet managed to look beautiful, wide-eyed and flat cheeked, her skin flawless, her eyes the colour of summer sky. Livia knew that her own eyes must be smudged with old make-up. She wiped around them with a greasy finger.

Tried to see her reflection in the window, but could only see a hollow-eyed shadow. She wished she could have a bath. She must smell. She was sticky hot – the air was too warm for a coat.

Tavius combed his hair, peering into the smoked glass. Marcus pretended to look out of the windows, but Livia could see he was looking at the girl.

Their speed increased and soon the speedometer above the driver showed 270 km an hour. On the other side of the canal, she could dimly see the flashing shapes of boats moving fast in the other direction.

At first, Marcus and Tavius tried to talk to the girl, but the effort of speaking over the crashing of the boat was too difficult. The bumping motion rattled their voices. Besides, the girl barely looked at them, noticed Livia with a slight smile. Livia was happy not to talk. Instead, she tried to take in everything she saw. Nothing she had seen in films on the digi had prepared her for the size of everything. The City rose into the sky like cliffs. Sometimes, between the moonscrapers, other older buildings cowered, dwarfed by their sleek neighbours. Between the towers snaked silver tubes, at many different heights, a maze of moving walkways like streams that carried people from building to building.

Eventually the boat slowed and turned into a narrow channel. As soon as it stopped, the girl pushed back the lid and they climbed out. She pulled some small blue coins from her pocket and counted some for the boatman. He had not once looked at the others. He didn't seem interested, his face blank.

'Follow me,' said the girl. How much more of this? wondered Livia. She was exhausted and hungry. Her eyes felt gritty.

More tunnels, just as before. In the light of the girl's torch, they could make out peeling pictures on the walls, patterns of tiles, arches and more tunnels to each side. They turned several corners before suddenly stopping. In front of them was a small wooden door. Slices of onions hung on strings above and to the side of it. There were more onion slices strewn thickly on the ground.

'Wait,' said Marcus. He took from his pocket the small bottle of oil Lochinvar had given each of them. The others did the same. They all sprinkled a few drops on their fingers and rubbed it under their noses, as Lochinvar had instructed. The powerful vapour took their breath away but they were glad of its strength.

The girl stared at them without expression.

Picking up a stone, she bashed on the door. There was a noise as someone on the other side opened it. The girl went in and the others followed.

2

The heat was overpowering after the coldness of the passages. Their nostrils filled immediately with the thick smell of roasting meat, sweat, and the sickly-sweet reek of illness. They wanted to hold their breaths. Livia found herself clenching her lips and breathing as little as possible. The sickness now seemed real, an invisible threat.

She held her fingers under her nose, inhaling the oil again. She wanted to keep her fingers there.

At first, their eyes could not take in what they were seeing. A vast hall, with a high vaulted roof. Dim electric lights strung from looping wires. A fire burning in the middle, its smoke hanging above their heads. Clothes on ropes draped across brick arches. Here and there a tiny splash of colour. Curtains across alcoves. Groups of chairs, mostly vacant. Random objects scattered or in piles, a plate, a cup, a book, a comb. Empty tables, abandoned spaces.

To the left a dying fire. A man stood poking with a stick at the smoking embers. Fragments of cloth refused to burn. Tears ran down his cheeks but he made no sound. Nearby, a small child, girl or boy, stood and stared and stared.

Further away, three children sat round a woman on a stool, listening to a story. One little girl kept looking at the fire and the crying man. The woman held the child's hand and gently took her finger and made her point at the page.

A musical instrument started up, halfway through a piece, as though their entry had interrupted it. The player, an old man, nodded to them as they passed, his fingers slowly strumming a sad melody on the lyre.

All the adults looked old, their skin grey. Most looked up and stared with hostile ashen faces as the newcomers passed. Even a mother with her young baby looked old. She sat in a corner, away from the others, limply rocking her wailing infant, and scowled at the visitors as they passed.

The four of them walked on, towards the main fire in the middle of the hall. The girl nodded to everyone and they nodded or smiled back at her. No one spoke to them or came near them.

The large fire sizzled with fat dripping from the carcass which turned slowly on the spit above it. Livia could hardly drag her eyes from the sight. It was, unmistakeably, a dog. Its spiralled tail still showed the charred remains of fur.

A thought came to her. This was how her parents had lived.

Near the far end of the hall, to the right, a ragged curtain hung across an opening in the wall. A long, thin trough sat in front of it, filled with glowing lumps of wood. The fire smelt strange, of something pungent, herbal. On the ground lay a large tray an inch deep with sliced onions. Onions hung from strings at the entrance. The racking sound of many people coughing rose from behind the curtain. And someone crying.

'Hurry,' muttered the girl. But as they passed, they could not help looking through a gap at the side of the curtain. They saw another enormous hall stretching ahead. Rows of people lay on thin mattresses, many with someone sitting beside them. Near the curtain a woman lay, clutching her stomach as she gasped for breath. Suddenly she turned on her side and vomited black liquid into a bowl. Beside her sat two other women, masks over noses and mouths, exhausted, dirty, thin. One held the woman's hand. The other read to her quietly.

They hurried on, sickened and afraid. Suddenly, their pungent oil didn't seem enough. Livia surreptitiously took a few more drops to her nose.

At the end of the hall, they came to another curtained opening on the left. The girl pushed it aside and they followed her. She closed the curtain after them. They followed her through a short passage to a long narrower hall with flimsy structures of wood and cloth along one side, like shacks. It was chilled and damp here, dimly lit by electric lights. A hollow dripping sound came from somewhere nearby.

'This is where we sleep.'

The girl led them towards one shack. On the door was a wrinkled paper sign with the words, beautifully written with curly edges and perfect spirals, *Cass's Place.*

She opened the door, leading them in. She switched on an electric lamp and they looked around. Four mattresses, a chair, a table with one leg propped on a block of wood, a large box, a hairbrush, a book open on the table. And shelves, full of books. Familiar as friends. Their ancient dusty spines cracked and hanging.

The smell of onion was strong and when Livia looked round she saw them. Peeled, hanging from the walls, and placed on the ground. 'Onions kill germs,' said the girl, watching her. 'Sometimes. Personally, I don't believe it, but we have to have them – it's a rule.' The back wall dripped with damp, and white mould sprouted from patches near the floor. The air was chilled.

'Leave your bags here,' said the girl. Putting hers down, Livia rubbed her shoulders. She felt space-headed with exhaustion now. 'This way,' said the girl again. Out of the shack. Where now? thought Livia. She just wanted to sit down. Eat and drink. Wash.

The girl knocked on the next door and they went in, though there was no reply. Inside was a wheelchair, rickety and ancient, its occupant a stick-skinny man wrapped in blankets. His face was grey and thin, his cheeks showing the skeletal shape of his skull. His eyes were closed.

'I've brought them, father,' said the girl.

His face lit up as he opened his eyes. 'I'm Milton,' he said, his voice dusty, wheezing. 'How wonderful to meet you. At last. You are all welcome. Very welcome.' He propelled his chair forward and held out his hand. As his eyes wandered over them, Livia realised he was blind.

Marcus and Tavius introduced themselves. Shook his hand.

'I'm Livia,' said Livia. His hand was cold and bony-dry. It felt as though it might snap if she squeezed too hard.

'Obviously,' smiled Milton. He bent forward in a spasm of coughing. Wiped his hand on the blanket. Livia flinched. Was this the virus? Was it safe to touch him? She clamped her lips shut, inhaled carefully through her nose, willing the virus to pass her by.

'I hope Cassandra has been . . .' – he stopped for breath – '. . . looking after you?' he said, when he had recovered. 'She has given you food? Drink?'

'Well, actually, no,' said Livia. She was too tired, too irritated, to cover up for the girl's rudeness.

'Cassie . . . where are . . . your manners?' said Milton. His breathing was quick, with no time for long sentences. 'Afraid my daughter . . . sometimes forgets . . . these niceties.' He paused. Sweat beaded on his forehead. Cassandra held a cup of water to his mouth and gently helped him drink.

'You need to rest,' she said, her voice soft, her hand behind his head. She brushed his hair away from his eyes.

'I must explain,' he said to the others. 'This . . .' he pointed to his chest. 'Not . . . the virus. Cancer. And this,' he pointed to his eyes, 'damned blindness – I told Cassie . . . not to tell the Poet. It would . . . upset him. Take them for food, Cassie, will you? And drink. We will talk later.'

Cassandra took them to her shelter again, collected cups and plates from a chest, and they went back into the main hall. The roasting dog had gone. She poured them something brown from a huge kettle that sat by the edge of the fire. And gave them bread, thick and heavy, but smelling yeasty and fresh. Slices of hard yellow cheese.

They carried their food back to Cass's Place. 'Pick a mattress,' she instructed. 'That's mine,' she added, pointing to one. They sat on their mattresses and ate. Livia found that her hunger had turned to nausea, but she needed to eat. She wiped a drop of oil around the edge of her cup. Cassandra watched her, contempt on her lips.

'It's very kind of you to give up your space,' said Marcus after a while. Livia's tongue curled at the edges.

'Yeah, thanks,' added Tavius, looking at her briefly and smiling.

'Yes, well,' Cassandra said, not looking at them. 'There isn't another place with room for four mattresses.'

'There's not much room,' said Livia. 'Shouldn't we . . .'

'I suppose you are used to more, aren't you? Well, it's the best we've got.' Cassandra snapped.

'That's not what I meant,' said Livia. 'I just meant . . .'

'Yes, well, as you can see, we don't live in luxury here. Not in a palace,' she sneered.

Marcus put his hand towards Cassandra, almost touching her arm. 'Hey, it's OK. We didn't mean anything. We know you've given up your space for us, and we're grateful. Really. Aren't we. Liv?'

'Yes, course,' Livia muttered. Why did this girl make her feel so small? She had only meant to be polite.

Well, who cares what the cow thinks?

'Don't suppose there's anywhere we can get a wash round here?' Tavius asked. Stupid guy, thought Livia – now he's going to get his head bitten off too.

'Yeah, sure. If you've finished eating, follow me.'

OK, so that's the way we're going to play it, is it? I get the picture.

'Bring your own towels. You've got them, I assume?' said Cassandra. Livia took some clean clothes from her backpack as well and, once more, they followed Cassandra as she made her way along the hall and through a doorway. A sign on the door warned, 'No persons with symptoms of disease'. They found themselves in yet another, smaller, vaulted hall. Damp crawled down the walls. Dripping water echoed through the hollow vaults. Along one wall was a series of cubicles formed by dirty curtains. Cassandra filled a bucket from a large tap on a pipe along the wall and fixed it to a contraption above one of the cubicles.

'Who's going first?'

'I'll go first,' said Livia quickly. She wasn't going to let the boys beat her this time. In the cubicle, which was bigger than she'd imagined, she undressed and put her clothes on a high ledge. She was standing on a wooden rack which formed the floor. Black oily water shone below. A sudden thought of rats made her shiver. 'OK, so what do I do?' she called, irritated at her ignorance. She felt exposed behind the flimsy curtain.

'Pull the rope when you're ready, just briefly to allow some water through the holes, then more later when you need it. Don't swallow it,' Cassandra added after a pause.

Livia obeyed. The shock of the ice-cold water took her breath away. At first, she could not have screamed if she had tried. Then the need to scream was overwhelming. She clamped her lips shut. She refused to make a noise. And as the water sluiced over her head she felt the thrill of one small victory. She could have sung.

There was a bar of mustard-coloured soap. She rubbed it to a thin lather and washed her hair. And as the water rinsed away the dirt of two days' travel, and the smoke and sweat, she felt warm and zinging and alive again.

She wrapped the towel around her, carefully making sure that it just, but only just, covered her breasts, and left the cubicle. Standing as tall as she could, bare shoulders back, legs straight, she stared Cassandra in the eyes. Livia was taller.

'Fantastic! Thanks, Cassandra. Where would you like me to get dressed?' she challenged, moulding a small smile onto her face.

'Wherever you like, Livia. Another cubicle, perhaps? Toilets over there if you need them. Boys over there,' and she pointed in a different direction. 'I'll see you all back at my place.' And she turned and left, her hips moving more than they needed to, thought Livia.

'What's her problem?' she asked.

'Hardly surprising, Liv — she's given up her space for us. What would you feel like?' said Marcus, watching Cassandra's retreating back.

Stung, Livia snapped, 'Yeah, well it's hardly our fault. She's just a grumpy cow, if you ask me.'

'Gorgeous, though,' said Tavius. Livia looked at him. She'd never heard Tavius notice anyone's looks before.

'Out of your league, Tav,' said Marcus.

'Oh don't tell me you've fallen for that! All that "don't touch me — I'm too beautiful" stuff?' said Livia.

'Touch of the green-eyed monster, Liv?' Tavius grinned, licking his fingers before smoothing his hair down.

'Oh, sure!' she snapped, furious. She left them to shower while she went to dress, shivering now in the icy air.

The silly episode had unnerved her. Her small sense

of victory as she had squared up to Cassandra now seemed pathetic. It felt wrong, amongst all this sickness and death and fear, to be so petty.

Listening to the boys' laughter, and their screams as the cold water hit them, she felt alone and helpless. The hopelessness of their task held her down. For a moment the boys' noise and the dripping and the rushing sound of water swept away into the distance and it was as if she was suddenly shut out of the world. She was the only one outside.

She walked back to Cass's Place, through the damp corridor. Outside Milton's door, she stopped. Held her hand up to knock, but then lowered it. Her heart began to beat faster. What could she say to him? If she were Marcus, she would have known what to say. If she were Tavius, she wouldn't have cared. She turned away, feeling foolish.

3

A little later that evening, people gathered around a fire in the main hall. There were about fifteen adults, tired-looking, quiet, smiling gently to each other in greeting. The children had gone to bed. Milton was there, his chair near the fire. He smiled at people as they arrived. He spoke quietly to the man who had been crying earlier and the man mumbled something and touched Milton's shoulder.

Some ate and drank, without seeming to enjoy it. Livia picked at a piece of salty, crackled meat with its fatless, gamey taste. Whatever it was.

She quickly wiped a drop of Lochinvar's oil around the edge of her cup before drinking. Cassandra looked witheringly at her.

Milton spoke, and everyone fell silent. 'Welcome, everyone. And especially, welcome to our guests.' Cassandra stood behind him, blank-faced, as he continued. 'They have come to us on another sad day. But they have come to help us. And we are grateful.' Livia noticed Cassandra's face tighten. There was a murmur which could have been welcome from the others, though most looked hostile. 'And now, let us eat and drink and be together. And let us have music, and stories, and show our guests how we live when times are good. As they will be again.'

The man with the lyre began to play and slowly people started to talk in groups. None came to speak to the newcomers. Livia took a sip of the drink she had been given. Some sort of home-made wine, thick and sweet. Marcus talked to Cassandra. Livia could hear his questions. He was asking how they had electricity and water. 'We're not useless,' Cassandra replied with irritation. It wasn't difficult to tap into the water supply, she added. And she told him how they had made their own electricity generator.

Marcus listened to her answers, his eyes bright in the flames, interrupting with more questions. Tavius lay back, his face blank and closed, listening perhaps to the music. Livia listened to all the voices as everyone relaxed into the wine, the warmth, the tiredness of their bodies.

She watched Marcus, seeing him in a new light. All her life she had not thought about their friendship. It was something ordinary, something she had never had to analyse. She had assumed, if she had ever thought about it, that it would always be there. Now, seeing him with Cassandra, she was not sure. He looked different. She felt different. As if he had moved from her space and she could now see him in focus.

The voices washed over her head and she shrank to a

pinpoint. She was invisible now. Something heavy and unbearably sad wrapped itself around her. She drummed her fingers on the ground and formed the chords inside her head.

The man with the lyre began to tell a story and everyone turned towards him. His singsong voice told the tales of ancient gods and heroes which she knew so well. But now, strangely, when she looked for a meaning she found none. She had never thought about it before. What were they for, these stories of the past?

What was the point? What was she here for? She felt unable to breathe properly and her legs were restless. She wanted to stand up and go somewhere else. Yet she couldn't, or people would notice. A voice spoke from behind her. She turned. It was Milton. 'Livia, would you take me back to my room? I feel tired.'

She stood up gladly and began to push his chair. Cassandra watched them go.

Back in his shelter, she enjoyed the chilled air after the thick heat and roasting smell of the main hall. 'Can I get you anything?' she asked. He turned his chair and his eyes wandered loosely over her face.

'Sit with me. Sit here,' and he pointed to the floor beside him. She took a cushion and sat down.

'I imagine you young people think you are too old

for stories?' His voice was wheezing but calm, his breathing better now.

'I suppose it depends on the story.'

'A story's a story. You can take what you want from it. And sometimes, all you have to do is store it in your heart. And it lies there and becomes a part of you. You never know what it's doing to you but it's there. Come closer. I need to touch your face.' She knelt by his feet. What was he talking about? The vagueness irritated her.

He put his hands slowly over the top of her head. She felt a rush of something, something almost fizzy washing through her body. Then his fingers, light as silk, touched and wandered all over her face, tracing every contour. Around the sides of her nose. Across her cheekbones. She closed her eyes and felt something soften in her heart. Her breathing slowed. His fingertips floated across her eyes and, after lingering there, returned to the top of her head.

'Everything is in the story. Everything always was. Listen to the story.'

'I still don't understand.'

'I don't know any more than that myself. I don't know the answers. But I know that when you need to know, you will know what to do. People like you always do. I can tell. I can feel your strength.'

Although his words were vague, she felt strangely

relaxed with his hands on her head and when he took them away it was as if she had lost something. She opened her eyes. His skin was wafer thin. As though it might be blown away in a breeze. A vein throbbed under his eye.

She wished the Poet could have been more like him. Or that her parents had waited around for long enough.

They could have put their hands on my head and I would have been calm. If they had just been there. If they had only stayed.
I wanted that. Wanted it from someone. I still do.

He spoke again. 'Listen to the story. Listen to the story in the heartbeat of the world. Listen to the heartsong.' And the poetry lulled her. Even though she could not have put its meaning into words.

Later, she was lying on her mattress, listening to the rustling and the wind in the tunnels and the distant coughing, when Marcus and Tavius came in. Without Cassandra.

They sat down cross-legged on the floor next to her. She breathed the familiar smell of them into her. But there was something unfamiliar too, something about their shadowed cheeks, their hardened faces. Perhaps it had been there before, but she had never noticed.

The future was seashore soft and edged with froth. Each time you looked at it, the tide had rushed in and changed it all.

'Well?' she said, forcing her voice to be light. 'Which of you is winning the contest of the golden apple?' She sat up, cross-legged, and picked a thread at the edge of her T-shirt.

'Contest, what contest?' said Tavius, his face without expression.

'She couldn't have me if she grovelled at my feet – I'm all yours, Liv, you know that,' Marcus replied smoothly. A strangeness shifted inside her. 'She does have great legs, though,' he added.

Livia hit him with a shoe and he grabbed her arms and pinned her down. She felt something rush through her. She had been this close to Marcus on countless occasions, but suddenly it felt different. Unexpected and new. A softness in the pit of her stomach. Hot blood in her heart. Speed in her veins. Her breathing quickened.

'Cut it, you two,' said Tavius. Marcus let go. Was there anything in his face, his eyes? Something in the way he moved further from her than necessary, in the way he did not look back at her? The blood thumped hard in her chest. She felt alive. But she was afraid, too. Part of her cried out for the way it had been before. The safety. Yet, another part of her did not.

She sat up, cheeks hot. Changed the subject quickly. 'OK, so, let's talk. What do you think of this – all this, these people?' she waved vaguely, speaking quietly.

'I don't know how they live like this,' said Tavius. 'God, I'd just give up.'

'You can see plenty of them wish we weren't here,' said Livia. 'There's one woman scowls every time she sees us.'

'Cassandra says some of them think we're going to make things worse. So far, the Pols haven't bothered to hunt them underground. The Pols are lazy and are quite happy shooting Outsiders on the streets every now and then. But some people think if we cause trouble, if we go to Center Tower and fail and the Pols think we're a threat, they'll come hunting. And they'll easily find them, some people say,' Marcus said.

'Oh, yeah, and what does Cassandra think?' said Livia, unable to keep her voice smooth.

A shadow fell across her vision. She looked up. Cassandra, standing in the entrance. After a pause, Cassandra spoke, looking directly at Livia, her sky eyes blazing.

'Cassandra thinks you're not up to it, that's what Cassandra thinks. Cassandra thinks you've had it easy up to now and you've waltzed in here like some Chosen Ones with your pathetic bottles of protective potion and you think you're going to change everything. Well, you've got a lot to learn. Boy, have you got a lot to learn!'

Livia stood up. A gust of anger raged inside her. She would have liked to grab Cassandra's perfect shiny hair and twist it round and round until her eyes watered and her head turned on its stalk. 'Just what exactly is your problem, Cassandra? We didn't choose to come here. But we're here now, whether you like it or not. Whether *we* like it or not. Obviously, I'd rather be back at home in my luxury "palace" than here in this stinking dump where no one seems to do anything except sit around and tell stories.'

Cassandra blazed back, her face inches from Livia's. Livia could smell her breath, like apples. Cassandra spoke, spitting. 'Yes, pathetic, aren't they? I don't need *you* to tell me that. But you haven't lived here. You don't know everything. A friend and I – we were going to find our way into Center Tower. We'd planned it all out. We didn't need you—' She stopped.

'And? So why didn't you do it then? If you can do it without us, why don't you?' spat Livia.

'They killed him. The Pols. They are allowed to use us as target practice – did you know that? They get bored otherwise. The Citizens are so dopey they can't be bothered to commit crime. Giving out parking fines and calling technics to fix broken moontrains makes the Pols hungry for a little bit of real excitement. He wasn't even doing anything!' Her blue eyes blazed. Her voice stretched tight and brittle-edged. 'He was standing watching the sun. That's all. He wanted to watch the sun set. I saw him die, saw them laugh as they watched his body fall into the canal and sink like . . . like rubbish.'

She turned away quickly. 'So, before you think you can swan in here and save us with the astonishing quality of your educated minds, think again.' She picked up a bag. 'I'm going for a shower. You know where everything is.' And she left.

The three of them looked at each other.

'Well, how was I to know?' said Livia. 'I'm not a mind-reader.' But she wished she had kept her anger in. The boys looked away. Marcus shrugged, his mouth tight, his face closed. He turned onto his stomach and began to do press-ups.

Tavius took out his tin whistle and began playing a quiet tune. The sound of home grated on her nerves.

'OK, so what do we do?' Silence. 'Marcus? How are we going to do this?'

'God knows.'

Why the shadow across your face, Marcus? Why the lips as thin as knives? She got to you, has she? We're supposed to be

127

friends, Marcus. We're supposed to be together. You're not allowed to go your own way.

And I thought . . . I thought something. I thought you felt . . .

We've been together all our lives. And now she slides in snake-like with her perfect hair and her baby-blue eyes and suddenly everything is different. She's a witch, Marcus. And you're weak if she's got you already.

Suddenly, now that it's important, I notice your weakness.

I thought . . .

I want . . .

'Tav? What about you? Shut that so-called tune. Have you got anything to contribute?'

'Can't say I have, Liv, no.' He was back in his shell. He continued fingering the whistle without blowing. She wanted to shake them both.

'Well, that's not much help, is it?' she snapped.

'I'm pretty bloody sick of the whole thing, actually, if you must know, Liv. It's not really what I expected. I'll just go along with whatever you do. Can't see there's much choice.' Tavius shrugged, looked at her, then closed his eyes, lying flat on his back, perfectly symmetrical, his face utterly blank, his dark hair falling away from his forehead in a tidy wave.

Marcus had finished his press-ups and lay on his back.

He spoke. 'Cass said tomorrow we're going to see how the Citizens live. See how the City works. It'll be cool.'

Oh, 'Cass' now, is it? Miss king perfect. Just because she has suffered doesn't make her special, does it?

It's not my fault her boyfriend died. And he's not the only person to have been shot by the Pols, is he? If only you knew, Marcus. She's not the only person to have lost someone that way. Not that my parents were there to watch the sunset, of course. They were there for a completely different reason. SO much better. So much more worthwhile. I don't think.

And what's it with Marcus and Tav now? Tav has contributed nothing. Plays that pipe as though he's nothing better to do. He's closed off. As if he doesn't care about anything – any of this – us.

Marcus. I don't know what's in his head any more. I used to know. Or maybe I just never looked before.

I thought we were all part of each other. Petals on a flower. Notes in a song. Atoms in a cell. I thought it was for ever, that I didn't have to think about it.

It's all changed.

And me? Have I changed? All I know is there's no way I can sit around reciting poetry and grubbing about in the filth underground. And yes, there is a hurry. Because exactly how much life do we have? If you know what you want to do, you

*have to do it NOW because later is too far away. Later may be
too late.*

*Why the sudden change of heart, when I said I wasn't going
to do this? Because I'm doing it for me, not anyone else. Least
of all not my parents who gave me away.*

*If I dig my fingernail into my ear lobe, really hard, really
really hard so it goes right in, the pain crashes over me like high
tide. It takes the rubbish with it and leaves the rest clean and
raked and sort of drifty. It takes my breath away and leaves me
floating somewhere warm.*

Livia lay awake long into the night. Silent. Angry. Her
mind spinning. Her thoughts refusing to rest. If she
could, she'd have made Marcus and Tavius get up and
dragged them and Cassandra to find this Center Tower,
right then, in the middle of the night. She burned with
the need to act now. Frustration gave her energy. Since
they were here, could they not just get on with it? She
couldn't breathe in this place, this dirty, airless dead-
zone, weighed down by the City above.

This need to act was new. Fuelled by something
burning. The ground under her feet was shifting again,
and she was fighting to keep her balance.

Part Four

Citizens

One half of the world cannot understand
the pleasures of the other.

Emma by Jane Austen

1

Next morning, after an unsatisfying breakfast of heavy bread and weak tea, Cassandra led Livia, Marcus and Tavius out of the hall.

Someone else had died in the night. The smell of the burning body seeped from the entrance to a tunnel at the far end of the hall. Tearful faces hurried by as people prepared for yet another grim ceremony. Livia sniffed the oil from her bottle, inhaling deeply. Cassandra looked at her witheringly as usual but Livia ignored her. If the smug girl wanted to catch the disease, that was her problem.

Cassandra spoke to them as they left the hall. 'Right. This is not a tourist trip. You need to learn how to get by up there. Good practice for when we go to the Tower. Do exactly what I say.'

She had already corrected their clothes. 'Leave your coats behind. You won't need them. And you might need to run.'

'You mean we're just going to walk about among the Citizens? Won't it be obvious we're Outsiders?' asked Marcus.

'Plenty of Citizens dress scruffily like this. Depends on their positions. It's your eyes and behaviour that will tell you apart. If anyone speaks to you, smile vaguely and pretend not to understand. Don't show anger, or fear, or anything at all. But remember, it's not illegal to be an Outsider. They'll ignore us as long as we don't affect their cosy little world,' she sneered.

'Apart from the small matter of the Pols using us as target practice,' said Livia.

'Yes,' said Cassandra, looking at her levelly. 'Apart from the Pols. But they won't usually do it in view of the Citizens. It might upset them.'

'How do the Pols tell who's an Outsider?' asked Marcus.

'They carry a scanner. Clipped to their wrists. It detects if you've no IDchip. Let's go.'

She unplugged a torch from a row connected to an electricity generator – and slung a small bag over her head and across her body, her arm muscles tight beneath a T-shirt. Her legs were slim and straight and long, tapering in dark-blue skin-tight leggings to halfway down her calves. Livia's legs felt heavy by comparison. She wished she hadn't spent so much time riding ponies.

She pulled her T-shirt down further over her hips.

Soon, after more tunnels and damp passageways, they found themselves looking through a metal grille high up in a wall. Beyond it was the City. Cassandra picked something off a ledge and held it to the grille. A mirror. She twisted it in different directions. 'OK, follow me, and fast.' In one smooth movement she pushed open the grating and swung herself out. Livia went next and Cassandra pulled her up, her small hand strong as steel. The boys followed and Cassandra replaced the grille. 'Right, walk. Don't make eye contact with anyone. Stay behind me. And when we get to the walkway, stand still.'

The three of them followed her, nervously. Along a narrow alley, round a corner. People, a sea of people. No one seemed to notice them. Where were the Pols? Faces approached, faces passed, faces bland and beautiful, faces painted. Livia was struck by the colours of the clothes and the hair, every shade of green and pink and blue and orange, as though a child had been unable to choose a colour and had just tipped everything into the painting. She was not used to such colour. She felt almost sick with it.

Around another corner. Cassandra turned her head and whispered, 'Walkway.' And suddenly beneath their feet the ground was moving. Tavius shot backward and nearly fell. Livia grabbed his arm. People looked at them, almost frowned. Cassandra glared.

Livia muttered to Tavius, 'Don't walk. Just stand still.' The walkway carried them smoothly forward. Livia turned. Marcus was grinning. She nudged him, frowning. Tavius was rigid with concentration, his teeth biting his bottom lip.

Through the people, they could see another river of heads moving smoothly in the other direction. They felt themselves travelling upwards, the slope becoming steeper, until the walkway became a moving stair. Soon they were in a see-through tunnel, the walkway level again, way above the street, the glass walls of the tunnel so thin that they might have been inside a bubble. The path forked ahead of them and some people were carried one way, some another. Livia looked down, dizzily. She saw a gleaming solatrain whiz beneath her feet. The space between them and the buildings seemed to be filled with a spaghetti system of tubes and walkways and stairs, entering doorways, rising and falling. Bubble lifts took people directly from one level to another.

And all the time, music. Piped and tinny, endlessly looped, sometimes jangly, sometimes calming. Every now and then the music quietened and above it came a sugary voice advertising the digi entertainment for that evening. Livia noticed that many people looked at their wrists when these announcements came. She could see silvery blue objects attached. She strained her head to see one on a neighbour's wrist. She knew what they were – mobes. They had all seen them on the digi but had never actually seen one properly. The expanda-screens really worked! When you looked directly at one, it appeared to grow to ten times its actual size, so that even though the screen was really no bigger than a large watch, it appeared much larger, reflecting itself in the surrounding air. She noticed someone watching her. Her heart racing, she looked away and resumed a bland face.

At first sight, almost all the people looked young, doll-like. Many wore skin-tight electrolon clothes sculpting their bodies. Some wore moulded nycra jackets fastened at the neck. Some had hair which didn't move as they swept along, its range of colours anything from sunflower-yellow to gazelle-beige, mint-green to ice-blue, and often striped or patterned in some way. Even the older ones had unlined faces and there was almost no grey hair to be seen, except the metallic silver on a fresh-faced young woman's head. The only way you could tell some were older was by the stretched unelastic look of their skin. A lack of glow. As though their youth was painted on.

Cassandra stepped off the walkway and the others followed. They were inside a building, its walls soft pink, with a shiny wet look to them. Livia wanted to touch them but she resisted. When she looked up she saw tiny things like flies' eyes set into the ceiling at intervals between the starry lights. Cameras, swivelling, following them. They felt watched. They could hear the hum of the air-purif, a fizz of electricity buzzing around them. Nothing else, no cars, no voices, no crashes of normal life. Dull silence, warm and soft and clean.

A machine whirred along the corridor towards them, its brushes sweeping the edges. It moved into doorways, hugging the corners, sucking up any dust it found. Behind it a green lemony liquid in a spray as fine as spiderweb fell on the floor. Suddenly the machine spoke. 'Take care now. The floor behind me may be wet. You are empowered to be responsible for your personal safety. See you later.'

Cassandra led them into a glass bubble. As they stood there, waiting for something to happen, a warm female voice warned, 'Please stand in the safety zone. You are empowered to be responsible for your personal safety.' Cassandra pointed to Livia's feet. She was not standing within the pink footsteps on the floor. She shifted her shoes into them and the voice said, 'Thank you! Take care now! See you later.' The glass bubble shot into the air. Involuntarily, Livia clutched at Marcus. He smiled back at her. His eyes shone with excitement, but Livia felt vulnerable, exposed by the glass, the cameras, the mysterious voices.

Out of the bubble and along another corridor, they followed Cassandra until she stopped at a door without a handle. A small sign showed the number T469.3 and the picture of an apple with a smiling face inside it. None of the doors had handles, they noticed. A camera whirred and fixed its eye on them. Cassandra didn't seem to try to avoid it. After a few seconds the door slid open and a boy stood there. Tall, streaky blond, with perfect golden skin and scared eyes. His neck was long and thin as if his head swayed on a stalk. He looked around nervously before letting them in.

'Come in quiet, Cass. Dad's a bit hyper. Need his pim scrip changed. Got anns next week. Hi,' he added, looking at the newcomers.

'Hi,' they repeated.

Livia held out her hand. 'I'm Livia,' she said.

He took her hand. 'Alex,' he said. His grip was lifeless. He was about to speak and then seemed to change his mind with a shrug.

'You 'splain, Cass,' he said, as they went inside. 'Like, you do it better'n me.'

'Alex is a Special,' explained Cassandra. 'And he's a good friend. He does what he can to help us. It's his com we use to contact the Poet.'

'How come we got in here?' asked Marcus. 'With the cameras?'

'I am registered through Alex's com so anyone I bring with me is accepted by the securi-syst. It's an eye-rec syst. Recognises eye-patterns. Ancient technology, but no one's come up with anything better. As soon as we came into the building I was recognised and accepted and you were with me so you were accepted too. Otherwise we wouldn't have got this far. Anyway, that's why there are no keys. If you are allowed in, you get in and if you're not you don't. Simple. Besides – I told you, Citizens mostly don't bother to commit crime. And Outsiders stay just that – outside.'

Alex was leading them through his apartment. The floors were silent, softly plastic, pumping wafts of warm air at their ankles. The air was the temperature of blood. There was a smell of strawberries and cream. And the walls changed colour, as if lit from behind with tinted lights. One moment gently blue, the next vibrant orange. 'They change with your mood, the walls,' said Cassandra quietly. 'They're no colour at all really – just the colour you make them in your head. It's the latest thing. Cool, isn't it?' She seemed different when she was

140

away from the other Outsiders. More relaxed. Softer. And she was clearly enjoying her role as guide.

A voice called out from a room. 'Zat you, Lexy?' A voice like warm milk, dozy, dreamy.

'Yes, Mum. Friends here, is all.'

'Kay. No prob. 'Member we're eating in Singapore, but.'

'Yeah, I know, Mum.'

Livia, Marcus and Tavius looked at each other. 'The virt-screen?' whispered Marcus. 'Can we see it?'

'Sure,' said Alex and he led them straight towards a wall. The wall opened and they found themselves inside a large room with pictures on three sides. The other wall was grey and glassy, but dull and thick, like a huge digi screen switched off. Alex pressed a button and suddenly the wall sprang into life. The whole front of a house appeared on the screen, trees swaying in the wind, the white-hot glare from the sun heating the room, people walking past the front door, wearing shorts and tiny shiny tops.

Alex fiddled with the control panel and a front door opened. Dizzyingly fast, they felt as though they were being swept through a mirrored front hall and along a passageway. Into a room, three sides open to the sea and sun, a table set for eight people, but with the nearest side of the table bare. A woman was bustling around, setting cutlery and mirrored glasses with stems as thin as silk, looped in twisted shapes like jungle vines.

Alex did something on the control pad and suddenly the woman spun round, looked straight towards them and beamed with delight as she straightened her skirt. 'Lexy! Hi! And you've friends! Come 'ere and give your aunt a hug!' The woman walked towards them and Alex met her and they seemed to hug in an odd not-quite-there sort of way, before she disappeared back into the wall, which sucked her in until she was on the other side again.

'Bye, Sall! See ya soon, kay!' said Alex, and with a press of another button the wall became a blank greyness again.

'Wow!' said Marcus. 'A virt-meet! It actually works!' He kept looking at the wall as though he could hardly believe what he had seen. He went over and examined the control pad.

'Totally unbelievable!' said Tavius. 'And you say they're in Singapore? That is just so cool. And you can go anywhere?' Livia had never seen him so animated.

'Gotta be linked but,' said Alex. 'Can't jus' get in any house, see. And if you wanta get someplace else, like I dunno cinema or you wanta shop, you haveta pay. Course.'

'What the hell?' A voice snarled behind them.

They spun round. Alex leapt towards the door.

A man stood there, naked from the waist up, his flesh soft and white and hairless. He held in his hand a gold-coloured bottle. Something dribbled down the side of his mouth. His thick black hair was slapped greasy over his forehead and his eyes blazed with fury.

'Lex!' he growled. 'Woss going on? Like, who're these? Get 'em out before I call the Pols, see.'

Cassandra spoke. Her voice entirely flat, bland. 'It's all right, Mr Cassidy. It's me. You remember. Cass. Friend of Lex's from Learnacy Center.'

'Get ya nice drink, Dad, kay?' said Alex quickly, and from a panel in the wall he pulled a cup, which he placed underneath a tap. Yellow liquid fizzed into it and Alex took two small containers from a shelf behind the panel and held each over the drink while pressing the tops. White powder splashed into the drink and he stirred it before handing it to his father, who took it and drank it without question. Within seconds his eyes were warm and glazed and a broad smile spread like butter across his sweaty face.

'Snice meet ya,' he slurred. 'Snice meet yall.' And he turned and left the room.

The visitors looked at each other. Alex was flustered. He looked away from them, fiddled with the panel in the wall.

Cass touched him on the arm. 'It's OK,' she reassured him. 'I'll explain. They'll understand.' And she turned to Livia and the others. 'They're Specials, too, but not as well-adjusted as some. Alex says they keep needing to take more funk – that's what the powder was, different powders for different effects – or his father gets agitated and his mum gets emotional. That was why Alex said they need their pim scrips – prescriptions – changed. They've got their anns – that's annual checks. Agitated and emotional are bad – you need to take drugs for agitated and emotional.' Alex did not seem to detect the sarcasm in her voice. She continued, 'Let's contact the Poet, Alex, shall we?' She spoke to him like a child, thought Livia. But she was gentle with him and he obviously trusted her.

He brightened up, and led Cass and the others out of the room, across a hall and through the sliding door into another room. Clearly his own room.

A digi screen dominated the room, occupying one whole wall. As they walked in, words appeared on the screen, neon and exploding like fireworks, 'Hi Alex! Hi Cass! And friends! Cool! How're u doing?!!' and a leaping frog went tumbling across the screen, grinning. Alex laughed and waved at the frog. The frog waved back.

'Whadya wanta do, Alex?' asked the frog.

'Vis-com, thank you, please, Freddie,' replied Alex, sitting down in front of the console.

'Sure, Alex! But first, did you take your pim today?'

'Yes, Freddie.'

'Well done, Alex! OK, now, vis-com here we go! Whodya wanta call?'

'Sorry, Freddie, I forgot! It's Cass wantsta call, but.'

'Sure, Cass! Hi!' Cass sat down in front of the screen, and tucked some stray hair behind her ear. 'Did you take your pim today?'

'Yes, Freddie.'

'You sure? You're lookin' kinda peaky.'

'I took it, Freddie. I promise.'

'OK, so whodya wanta call? Do I have the address databased or is it a new buddy?'

'Mr Shelley, please.'

'Okey dokey, here we go! Bye for now Cass! See ya later! Take care now!' And the frog hopped away to the edge of the screen where it reclined in a lounger, wearing sunglasses and sipping a tall drink. A picture of a dandelion appeared in the centre of the screen, and the seeds blew away one by one. They watched them floating off in random paths. Suddenly, the screen exploded into a cascade of stars and yellow fizzling specks. And a face appeared. The Poet. Smiling, his long grey hair combed and soft around his face like a halo.

'Cassandra! And is that Livia? And the boys?' Something misty in his eyes. Something thick in her throat. Livia felt a world away from the castle and its endless skies and swaying trees and fresh air. She had a weird moment of detachment, a feeling of being nowhere. What floor was she on? She had no idea. There was no window in the room, no window that she had seen anywhere in the flat. She felt a dizzying sense of unreality.

'Good morning, Mr Shelley,' said Cassandra. 'I hope you are well.'

She's as bad as Marcus. The politeness. The talking to adults bit. And why does the Poet want to speak to her?

'Good day, Cassandra. I hope you are well. May I speak to Livia, please?'

Hah! See?

Cassandra moved off the seat and Livia sat down, settling her body into the cocooning squishy material. She smiled. 'Hi PB!' she said.

'Now, Livia, just because you are a long way away does not mean you can be disrespectful.' But he didn't look angry.

146

'Sorry, Mr Shelley.' The routine, the schoolgirl stuff. Reassuring as a blanket, as hot chocolate, as stories round the fire.

Take me back. Take me back. Say the whole idea's off. Say it was all a mistake, all a joke.

Give me more time. One day I'll be ready. I thought, for a while, that I was. But seeing you, seeing home . . . It's taken it all away again. And brought all the rest back. The uncertainty.

I'm sorry I didn't say goodbye properly. Sorry the words wouldn't come. Why is it so easy to say what I feel in my head and so impossible to say it out loud?

This is weird. I didn't know this was how it would be. I thought I didn't care about . . .

'How are you managing, Livia? And how is Milton? Did you find the place all right? Are they looking after you? What do you think of everything? Are you being polite and helpful to everyone? And Cassandra, she's nice, isn't she? And what about the virus, the disease? Is it as bad as we thought? Are you using Lochinvar's oils? He told me to ask you. And Center Tower – do you have a plan?'

Too many questions. She wanted to tell him everything, tell him about the roasting dog, the freezing water, the underground reek of bodies and damp and

147

filth and death, the skeletal wheezing figure of the blind Milton, the weakened dying people, the stench of the burning body that morning, the hopelessness of their task. But with Cassandra and Alex there, how could she? She wanted to tell him that she felt alone and confused and frightened. But with Marcus and Tavius there, how could she?

'It's cool, Mr Shelley. Everything's . . . like, cool.'

'Livia, for goodness' sake. You can do better than that. You sound like a Citizen.'

I want to tell you, tell you properly. But something happens inside when I talk to you and I become the child I was. Like a half-finished sculpture that has escaped from its creator. I am running across the floor, dissolving, my edges melting into liquid clay.

You irritate me, confuse me, shake the water I stand on. You make me feel small so I act small. You want me to be something. But I am not the something you want. I want to be myself but that's not the me you want.

Who am I? Not a Citizen. Not who I was. Not an Outsider, and yet an outsider.

The broken pieces of wood are floating on the waves behind me. The ship is falling to pieces and I don't know whose it is.

Bite my lip, hard. Until it doesn't hurt. Any more.

'Totally, Mr Shelley!' she said, teasing. 'There's a thing that cleans the corridors and it speaks to you! And walkways so you don't have to make an effort to move. And we saw a virt-screen – we saw a woman in Singapore preparing a meal that the people who own this flat we're in are going to share. We could feel the heat, smell the flowers. And we saw how great the funk is – Alex's father was so totally stressed out and when he took some funk he just went all calm and happy. Alex is going to let us have some!'

She turned and smiled at Alex and winked. Cassandra frowned. Marcus grinned. Tavius raised his eyebrows.

Livia enjoyed the feeling of control. She was irritating the Poet, she could see, and Cassandra. And at the same time, she was playing on the same side as Marcus and Tavius.

'Livia, remember everything you have been taught! Remember you are part of something greater, something worth more than a few moments of pleasure. Remember what I told you!' His face had an urgency to it, his steely eyes shining brighter than usual.

'Sorry. We've got to go now.' She turned to Alex and mouthed the words, 'How do you turn this thing off?'

The Poet was speaking. 'Take care, Livia, boys, Cassandra. Take care.' Alex stood in front of the screen and waved. The Poet's face disappeared.

'So cool,' said Tavius, staring at the screen, now showing a troop of frogs dancing to the beat which drummed around them from invisible speakers. Glitzy adverts appeared around the edge of the screen, pumping their neon colours.

'How do you turn the whole thing off?' asked Livia.

'Can't,' said Alex. 'You turn off sound when you wanta sleep. Other times, it's on, but. Like, why'd anyone want it off?'

Livia looked closely at him, trying to work out whether he was serious. Something told her that he was. Cassandra was looking at her, judging. Livia stared back, for just long enough, then looked away.

2

'Tell us about the funk, Alex,' said Tavius.

'Funk? It's stuff. You put it in like a drink. Pends how you feel, like tense or things. You take the right stuff and you feel kay. You wanta try?'

Marcus looked at the others. For a moment, no one said anything.

'Yeah, sure.'

'Cool,' said Tavius. Livia looked at them both. What were they playing at? Surely they weren't really going to do this? She hadn't meant it seriously. To joke about it was one thing, but really to do it? They seemed to have forgotten everything they were there for. And did Tavius have any words in his vocabulary other than *cool*?

'No!' said Cassandra, angrily. 'You don't know what it will do. You've never had it before.'

'Oh come on, Cass, it's only for research! It's important we understand, isn't it? How can we understand what we're up against if we don't experience what the Citizens call happiness?' Marcus stared straight at her.

'You don't understand. It takes away your will power.'

'What, with just one taste? I bet I'm stronger than

that. And it wears off, doesn't it? I mean it's just for a while? Isn't it, Alex?'

'Sure, like an I can give you a lil bit, just. Won't last long.'

'Alex, you stupid fool, don't you dare! Don't be more stupid than you need to be!' The venom in Cass's voice was sudden. Alex looked stung. He blushed, flustered.

'But you . . .'

'Shut up!' She glared at Alex so hard that it was as though she was overpowering him with her will, with the violence of her thoughts. An idea came into Livia's mind, flashed there suddenly.

'You've taken it, haven't you?' she accused Cassandra.

There was a pause. 'So? I took it once. I wish I hadn't.'

'So how can you tell *us* not to?'

'Maybe because I know more than you!' Cassandra snapped.

'Don't you think we should discover for ourselves?' asked Marcus.

'Just once,' added Tavius. 'It can't do us any harm. Everybody takes it. There's no law against it. There'd be a law against it if it was bad for you.'

'Livia?' asked Marcus. 'What do you think?'

Cassandra butted in. 'Suit yourselves. What would I

care? You think you know it all, so the sooner you find out you don't the better.' She went over to a cushion and sat down, cross-legged. She plucked a tiny s shaped object from where it sat stuck as if magnetically to the wall, and fitted it over and into her ear. She adjusted a remote control that was also attached to the wall and shut her eyes, drumming her head to whatever beat she was hearing. Her fury was in the rigid shape of her jaw and the way her fingers beat against the floor.

Alex looked at her. 'I dunno . . .' he said. 'Like, Cass is my friend but, see?'

'But it won't do any harm, Alex. It's just funk. People take it every day,' said Marcus. 'Liv? You up for it?'

Livia was only mildly interested in what funk would be like, but her choice was simple. Whose side was she on? Was she with Marcus and Tavius or with Cassandra? Whom did she want and need more? And when Marcus looked at her like that, straight in the eyes, with that smile that went right through her . . . She was still not used to the sensation, was still trying to work out whether to trust it.

'Sure!' she said. Cassandra still had her eyes shut, clamped shut. What was she worried about? Livia had already realised that Cassandra was volatile, full of anger and emotion behind her façade of cool control. But wasn't she over-reacting a bit? What was behind it?

Livia brushed the doubt aside. She was with Marcus and Tavius again. The feeling of belonging was soft.

'Kay,' said Alex, looking once more at Cassandra and then ignoring her. Her eyes remained shut. 'First, we gotta make the mix, see?' He sat in front of the screen and the frog leapt up and greeted him. The same routine as before. Livia already found the frog's empty friendliness and Alex's obvious enjoyment irritating.

When he asked for a 'funk mix prog', a new screen appeared. 'Who's first?' croaked the frog.

'You go, Livia,' said Alex.

'What do I do?'

'Nothing. Watch Freddie just. His eyes.' Livia watched the frog as it danced up to her and stared. It looked slightly puzzled, putting its head on each side as it seemed to look inside her. Then it did three back flips and the screen showed some colours and numbers. There was a red blob followed by the number four and a green blob with the number five.

Alex looked at her. 'Wow! Weird!' he said. 'Kay, Marcus.' Marcus went through the routine. The screen showed blue followed by the number three, and green followed by six. Alex shook his head wonderingly. Tavius' score was 'yellow one'.

'Smore like it,' said Alex. 'Like, you don' need a thing, see?'

'What does that mean?' asked Tavius.

'Means you don' need funk, so. You're kay with not.'

'Oh, come on,' said Tavius, his chocolate eyes pleading. 'You can't let me miss out. That's not fair!'

'Won't do any harm, spose.' Alex opened a panel in the wall and took out three silver glasses. Pressing a spout he allowed a small amount of clear fizzy liquid to fall into the glasses. He then took various silver containers with coloured lids and held them over the drinks, pressing the top a certain number of times. He passed the correct glass to each of them.

They looked at each other.

'What are we waiting for?' asked Marcus. 'Cheers!' And he took one mouthful and then tipped the drink down his throat. Within seconds, as Livia and Tavius watched, his vision seemed to float away into somewhere else. His eyes were not exactly spinning, but no longer firm and steady. No longer challenging and bright. The muscles on his face seemed to blend and relax. Almost as though the life went out of him. He sat down.

'What's it like?' asked Livia, fascinated and frightened equally.

'Nice,' he said blandly. 'You coming?' And his smile was soft and irresistible.

Livia and Tavius looked at each other. There didn't

seem to be any reason not to. As Livia drank the sweet fizzy drink, she saw Cassandra watching her and then closing her eyes once more and retreating into her music.

Livia sat on the soft bubblegum floor and sank into it.

For a few seconds, she thought nothing had happened. But then she realised that there was an emptiness at her centre. Hard to explain. Something like a soft white blanket had been thrown over whatever was there and she couldn't feel it any more. Like having a dream where you know you've broken your arm, but the pain just isn't there. You know you are supposed to feel something but you just don't. What had been there before, in that peaceful blanked out place in her head? She couldn't remember.

Her body felt completely normal. At least the outside bits did. But inside she was only half of herself. But it was a nice half. Calm and happy. And then she realised what wasn't there. Anger. When she thought of her parents, of the Poet, of the miserable conditions of the Outsiders, of the task she had been set, none of it mattered any more. None of it hurt, none of it burned. Like watching a storm from inside a house, wrapped up and warm.

It was amazing. This lack of anger. This floating above herself, this . . . well, there was no other word but happiness. It was as if the only word was *yes*. The world had no *no* left in it.

She could see Marcus and Tavius. She was talking to them. But what she said was not important.

She saw Cassandra sitting cross-legged and wondered why she looked so angry, drumming her fingers to the beat of something only she could hear.

This is what my life could have been like. Every day. Warm and looked after. This is what life is like for the Citizens. This is what my parents turned away from. Funny that. How odd. Never mind.

It doesn't matter. Nothing ever did.

Imagine what amazing wonderful brilliant songs I could play if I was this happy. Imagine their beauty and their power!

If I try it now, if I drum my fingers, feel the chords . . . . but there's nothing there. I see the beat, could name the rhythm, but I don't feel it. Where has the feeling gone? I liked the feeling. It was me. I loved the sound and the fury. Now it sounds like an idiot speaking. Now it signifies nothing.

That reminds me of something. But I can't remember what. Something I read once. Never mind.

What's wrong with Tavius? He's gone all floppy. Is he asleep?

'Marcus? What's wrong with Tav?'

Marcus shook Tavius' shoulder. Cassandra leapt to her feet and the music tube fell from her ear onto the floor, where it lay drumming its tinny beat into the room.

'Shit, what have you done! You bloody fools!' she shouted. She slapped Tavius' face. He barely seemed to notice. He was an icy grey colour, his lips drained of blood. His eyes were open but he didn't appear to be seeing anything.

Marcus and Livia watched, fear creeping steadily towards them as they struggled to push away the effects of the funk. Livia felt a peculiar sensation that her brain was not part of her body. Her brain was telling her that Tavius was in trouble but her body was refusing to react. It refused to feel fear.

Cassandra pushed Tavius down so he was lying flat on the floor. She raised his feet onto a chair. She slapped his face again and shouted at him. Still his face looked grey. His breathing was slow and shallow, almost imperceptible. Several times Livia thought it was going to stop altogether.

'Alex, bring me an upper – now!' Alex disappeared and came back a few seconds later with a tiny plastic object which he passed to Cassandra. With a flick and a twist she ripped off the lid and, pressing Tavius' mouth open with one hand, she squeezed the contents under his tongue.

There was no response. Now, for the first time, Livia felt real fear flooding towards her. She looked at Marcus. His face was white, his cheeks rigid. His hair was across his face, a strand caught in his mouth. He moved his hand and gripped hers. It was all they could do. Cassandra was the only one who was able to act.

Within a few more seconds, the colour came back to Tavius' face and he shook his head. He tried to sit up but Cassandra pushed him back down.

'What happened?' he asked. His arms were twitching. His breathing now fast. 'I need to sit up!' he shouted. Livia had never heard Tavius shout in anger before. There was irritation in his eyes as he pushed Cassandra's hand roughly aside and sat up.

'You shouldn't have taken anything. I told you,' she said. 'I said you didn't know how it would affect you. Alex, were you careful with the measurements? Alex!'

Alex was pouring something into a cup. Dropping some powder in. He drank from it, quickly.

'Wasn' my fault, Cass, but. Honest. Anyway, doesn' matter now, doesn' it? Like, everything's fine, see?' He smiled at Cassandra, puppy-like, almost cringing. He drank some more, tipping the cup back.

'It was my fault! All right?' said Tavius. 'Don't blame

him. The flaming frog said I didn't need anything but I said I wanted it. OK? So blame me if you need to blame anyone.' His breathing was still fast and his legs twitched.

'You mean you came out as yellow one and you still took something?'

'Sure. So? How was I to know what it meant?' he said angrily. 'What does it mean, anyway?'

'Yellow one means that you are as calm and controlled as it's possible to be without funk. Funk will lower your blood pressure. You probably already have very low blood pressure, so you passed out.'

Livia spoke. She felt like a small child caught doing something wrong. 'But it's OK now, though. Thanks to you, Cassandra,' she added, with difficulty.

'Do you think we should go now?' asked Marcus, looking unnerved. Suddenly, the room with its strange gadgets didn't seem so interesting any more. The strangeness was now sinister, hostile. The frog on the screen sat in a corner and stared at them. As though it was watching, and thinking. The background music, turned down as far as it would go during waking hours, jangled their nerves.

'No,' replied Cassandra. 'I'm afraid that now we can't go.'

'Why?' asked Tavius. He struggled to his feet and

moved towards the door. His arms wouldn't stay still and he was chewing his lip. His hair, normally so tidy, was sweated to his forehead and he did nothing about it. His wild eyes flicked from side to side.

'Because you are in no state to go. Look at you. You'd be spotted within minutes, behaving like that. You'd be a risk to the rest of us. And to yourself,' she added under her breath.

At that moment the frog swelled to fill the centre of the screen.

'Hi Alex! Your mum's coming! Wonder what she wants!'

Alex moved to his feet as the door slid open.

A woman stood there, smiling. Her wispy hair framed a round face. Her skin was like soft wax. She seemed at first to be wearing very little – they could see her flesh from her ribcage to below her hips, but when Livia looked more carefully she could see that in fact a skin-coloured electrolon garment covered her, pulling in the flesh so that no bulges or creases appeared. She wore peach-coloured slicks to halfway down her calves and her ankles were perfectly hairless, tanned and soft-skinned. Her feet shuffled in fluffy slippers of egg-yolk yellow.

'Come n help Mum with the food, Lexy?' she said. 'Everything's in the shute now. Everything you asked for! Need your help to get it all ready, but. Lo, everyone,' she said warmly, seeming to notice the others for the first time. 'Nice to see ya. Kay, Lexy, five mins, kay?' And she turned smoothly and walked driftily away, leaving the scent of butterscotch in the air.

'Sorry, y'all. You gotta go, so.' Still relaxed from the funk he had taken when Cassandra snapped at him, Alex looked entirely unworried. His face was like a doll's, unmoving.

Livia looked at Tavius. 'How are you feeling?'

'Fine. Let's just go. I need some fresh air. It's stuffy in here. Can't breathe properly,' he said, an edge to his voice that Livia had never heard before today. She and Marcus looked at each other. Marcus had been unusually silent. Livia felt a vague unease. She could still feel the edges of the warmth and softness she had felt only a few minutes before, but it was now tinged with sharpness. And something very much like panic, struggling to take over. She tried to control her mind, to be in charge of herself again. But she felt detached. Still vaguely dreamlike.

'Right,' said Cassandra. 'Seems we've no choice. We'll have to go and just hope to hell nothing happens. You'll all have to be extra careful, concentrate. Livia, you walk behind me, then Tavius, and Marcus at the back. Fix your faces as before, no eye contact. And listen for my instructions. This is not a game. This is for real. Got it?'

Feeling small, the three of them nodded. Even Tavius was silent, though he still seemed tense. Jumpy. His eyes darting. Every now and then a manic expression would flash across his face, and disappear just as suddenly.

As they went back down the corridor, Livia thought of Alex's face as they had left. How he had smiled his bland, milky smile, as though nothing had happened. And then there was Cassandra, tight-jawed and furious. She was the one who had acted; she was the one who was alert enough to know what was going on. Yet Alex was the one who was happy and calm, with everything he needed. Who was suffering? Who was happy? She didn't have the answers and she was only just beginning to understand how complicated the questions were.

Back on the moving walkways once more, Livia concentrated on keeping her face blank, not meeting anyone's eyes. They were swishing past rows of huge glass windows, with bright lights inside. She recognised this as an entertainment zone. She had seen them on the digi, but nothing had prepared her for the spangling glitziness of them. People stood or sat at consoles, in front of machines that seemed to sing and dance at them. Staff walked around with enormous smiles pasted on their faces, carrying trays of multi-coloured drinks and desserts. And in some windows there were robo-waiters, gliding around with glass boxes filled with sweets or ice creams.

Through one window, they saw people dancing under fireworks. Livia knew what this was: an aquaoptic shower, powerful razor-thin jets of precision-propelled water carrying coloured light. As the aquaoptics arced to the ground, it looked like rain on fire.

In another window, a woman lay on a white table, fully clothed, while around her floated enormous angel-fish and butterflies and sunflowers. The woman raised her hand to catch them, but her fingers closed around nothing. When a striped parrot-fish hovered above her face, the woman smiled and blew gently and the fish floated up and became a butterfly. Livia knew this was all illusion. It was a relaxatank. An expensive experience, but floating in a virtual dreamworld was supposed to be worth the price.

She heard a commotion behind her, harsh in the background music. Marcus was urgently whispering, 'Liv! Liv!'

She turned round. Tavius had stopped. He was standing, staring rigidly at something. He licked his lips, as though his mouth was dried.

Pols.

3

Two of them. Sitting on a bench. Even if Livia had not seen pictures, she would have known they were Pols. Sheathed in tight black from head to toe. Heads enclosed in black rubber hoods, with black sunglasses hiding their eyes. Black boots with metal tips. A silver zip running diagonally from one shoulder to the opposite hip. Clipped to their wrists flashed the scanners which could identify people with no IDchip.

And, nestling under one arm, the metallic blue glint of their tiny weapons. Tiny but deadly.

The Pols looked up. Turned their wrists. Looked straight towards Livia and the others. Smiled. Stood up. Cass had turned round, had seen what was happening. 'Follow me!' she whispered, urgently. 'Quick!' And she grabbed Tavius and pulled him along. Marcus and Livia followed, hurrying without running, following Cass as closely as they could. They wove their way between the other people, trying not to bump into them, trying to hurry without seeming to.

Cassandra jumped off the walkway and onto an escalator going down. The others followed. The escalator crawled. Cassandra looked over her shoulder and Livia saw her face, tight with fear. At the bottom,

Cassandra turned sharp left. Faster now, they ignored the startled eyes of passers-by. Shouts from behind. Livia snatched a look over her shoulder. The black figures of the Pols were not far away. They were grinning. Citizens stood aside to let them pass.

Round another corner, street level. Open air. Fewer people here. They began to run. Cassandra was dragging Tavius. His face was hot with exertion, his breath loud rasps. Marcus grabbed his other arm and they ran. They didn't look round.

They were in almost empty streets now, grimy grey with narrow alleys off to each side. Livia's breath was rough in her throat, her heart racing, her face blood-hot. She could see that Tavius was flagging. Marcus stumbled. Livia's heart crashed. Cassandra looked round, fear on her face.

Round one more corner, Cassandra stopped suddenly and pulled Tavius into a narrow side alley. 'Quick! In here!' And they found themselves running down an alley so narrow they could only go in single file. Livia was last. Her back felt exposed, cold. She imagined being shot from behind, could almost feel them taking aim, squinting down the barrel, pulling the . . .

Suddenly, Cassandra slid to a halt, pulled them behind some boxes stacked high. A grating in the wall, low down. 'Help me,' she gasped. She and Marcus dragged the grating away from the wall. Cassandra went through feet first and held out her hand for Tavius. Then Livia and finally Marcus slid through the grating. Livia felt a sharp knife-like pain in her ankle as she landed.

A wave of blackness washed over her and she clenched her face in a silent scream as she crumpled to the ground. Cassandra's foot trampled on her hand. Tears squeezed between her eyes but she made no noise.

'Shit, Livia, what are you doing down there?' snapped Cassandra.

'Nothing, just slipped.' She forced the words evenly between her teeth. If she controlled her breathing, if she trapped the air in her chest, she could manage not to show she was in pain. She stood up, tried to put her foot down. Pain, sharp, sliced through it.

'What do we do now?' asked Marcus.

'We wait here. Till we can be sure they haven't followed us, then we go back, onto the streets again and back to the entrance to the tunnels.'

'Where are we?' Livia managed to ask. She had assumed this was another entrance to the tunnels. How could they go back onto the streets?

'This is the basement of an old building. We are in a fairly dead part of the City. Old buildings, old streets, not many solacars. And no moving walkways. Citizens like moving walkways. A few old-fashioned shops, bit of sleazy entertainment, stuff for the poorer Citizens. And the shops take cash, so we can buy things and no one much minds. And we can sell moonstones.'

'Moonstones?' asked Livia. Anything to take her mind off the pain in her ankle.

'Coal. The Citizens have never heard of coal and they think these shiny black things contain the "spirit of the universe". Ask them what that means and they wouldn't have a clue, but they just believe us when we say they have a special magic. It's how we make money.'

'You can't make much like that,' said Marcus. His voice sounded tense and thin. He was frightened. Livia needed Marcus not to be frightened.

'We don't need much. Other things we find. Or steal.' Livia could see Cassandra's eyes challenging, her face grey in the light from the grating. But she had no intention of taking up a challenge. Livia had begun to see that Cassandra knew more than she ever would about how the City worked. 'Things fall off the back of solatrucks. We take what we need. Some shopkeepers give us damaged food. We fish from the canal. And we hunt.'

'Hunt?'

'Dogs and rats mostly. Don't bother with cats. They're too thin.'

There was a silence. In the distance they could hear the voice of the City, grinding and clanging. No footsteps passed the grating. After a while, Cassandra said, 'Right, time to go. We go back along this alley, turn right at the end. But then we should split up. Use the walkway but stay at the edge so you can jump off at the second turning right. Take that turning. There's no walkway. About eighty metres along that street, on the right, is our grating. Just past a bright red doorway. Everyone got that?'

They all nodded. They would do exactly what she said, afraid of making another mistake. Next time they might not be so lucky. Cassandra continued. 'When we separate, I'll go first. Then Livia. Then Tavius. Then Marcus. And Marcus – stay close to Tavius. Either the funk or the upper will be wearing off by now and it's impossible to say what he'll be like. And everyone, walk slowly. Unless you see the Pols. If they see you, run like hell.'

She pushed the grating away and climbed out. Livia went next, with Marcus helping her up. Pain shot through her foot when she put it down. But she could deal with it by breathing over it. She helped pull Tavius up. He was completely silent, withdrawn into himself. She touched his shoulder. He stared at her. He looked ill and frightened and lost somewhere. She wanted to put her arms round him. But you didn't do that with Tavius. She wanted to tell him that it would be all right. But she couldn't say it.

Once Marcus was up and the grating was back in place, they set off along the alley towards the light at the end. Livia glanced up. She saw the milky sun in a pale blue sky. It looked unreal, somehow, not like the sun back home.

If she walked slowly, she could manage not to limp. She refused to limp. She refused to let any of them, especially Cassandra, see that she was hurt. It would be a challenge, she decided. If she could manage to get all the way back without them noticing, she could be proud of herself. Focusing on breathing, focusing on putting one foot in front of the other, evenly, helped her not be frightened. The fear was there, but she could force herself to ignore it.

At the end of the alley, Cassandra carefully looked in both directions. She turned back to them, 'OK, I can't see them. They've probably given up. Follow at a distance, Livia, and watch me.' Livia nodded. She watched Cassandra walk casually to the walkway and step on. There were very few people on it. They didn't notice her. No sign of the Pols. Livia took a deep breath and followed. She kept her eyes fixed on Cassandra's black hair. She strained her ears for any out-of-the-ordinary noise or shouting. She turned round to make sure Tavius was following. He was.

So far, so good.

Suddenly, without warning, the fear rose like a wave in her chest and her breathing quickened. Get a grip, she told herself. Calm down, slow down. The panic moved away and sat waiting in a corner of her mind.

Cassandra had disappeared. The panic grew again. But then Livia remembered – second turning right. She leapt off the walkway just in time, knocking against a woman. For a moment, Livia just stood there, not knowing what to do, not knowing if she should say sorry or not. What was right in this weird place? But the woman just drifted past, her face bland.

Livia took the turning. She could see Cassandra removing the grating eighty metres ahead. Saw her climb in feet first. Nearly there. Her breathing quickened again as she realised how close she was. She would soon be safe. She turned back to see if Tavius was following her.

He wasn't.

4

Livia stopped. Should she go back? There was still no sign of him. For Christ's sake, hurry up Tav! The end of the street was empty. Suddenly, she saw him. He was at the very end of the street, moving slowly. Backwards. Staring at something which she could not see. He stopped when his back was against the wall. And stood there. His eyes were fixed ahead.

Livia knew he must have seen the Pols. He had frozen. She didn't stop to think. She ran back to him as fast as she could. 'Tav!' He didn't seem to hear her. In seconds she had reached him. Grabbed his arm. Tried to pull him with her. His face was white and rigid, his eyes rabbit-wide. He pointed. She followed his arm. Pols, the same two, on the other side of the street. Not looking at them. They seemed to be scanning the passers-by. At any moment they would see Livia and Tavius.

Where was Marcus? He was nowhere to be seen. It was all going wrong. She whispered in Tavius' ear, soothing. 'Tav, it's OK. Come with me. We have to go back. Back home. We have to follow Cassandra. Everything will be fine.' She found herself speaking very calmly, as if to a frightened child.

She felt his muscles loosen slightly, sensed him softening. She gently pulled him but kept a close eye on the Pols. Still no sign of Marcus. Where the hell was he? One of the Pols stopped. He was looking straight at them. Livia froze. She felt Tavius turn stone-like again. Maybe the Pol wouldn't see, wouldn't recognise them.

But he nudged his companion. They had seen. Livia could have run then, could have escaped. She was nearer the corner, nearer safety. She *wanted* to run. She wanted to run and never come back.

The Pols began to smile.

'Tav!' she whispered in his ear. 'You have to come with me! You have to run, NOW!' she hissed desperately, pulling him towards her just as the first Pol fired. A bullet twanged off the wall inches from her head. She felt its breath. As she hurled herself round the corner, dragging Tavius, she felt him being hit, felt the jerk of his body as the bullet smashed into him, heard the gasp of his breath as he realised. Eyes wide with horror, she watched as a shocking poppy of blood spread across his arm.

And in that instant she knew there was nothing more to lose and the fear exploded as she shouted, 'RUN!' and dragged him with her. Round the corner. Along the alley. He stumbled behind her. Fear and pain gave her extra strength. She didn't look behind. There was nothing else she could do but run with him.

Cassandra's face stared up at them from the grating. 'Thank God!' she said. 'Quick! Get down here!'

'Tav's been shot,' said Livia. 'His arm.' They bundled him down into the darkness and Livia slid through after him. She ripped off his torn sleeve and folded the material into the thickest pad she could. 'Lie down, Tav,' she said, and she pressed the pad against the wound. She tied it on tightly with her belt. She couldn't see what it was like, but it would have to do. 'Press your hand on it,' she told him. Silently, he obeyed. 'You OK?' she asked.

He shook his head. 'I'm sorry, Liv,' he said. His voice was tight and thin, shaking as if with cold. She gripped his hand. It was limp in hers.

Cassandra was looking through the grating. 'Where's Marcus?'

'I don't know. He was behind me and then he wasn't,' said Livia, pushing a new fear away. He would come. He must be coming now. She strained for the sound of his footsteps. He would come, wouldn't he? He would just be waiting his chance.

Everything was falling to pieces. What would the Poet think? They had failed even before they had begun. They had been nothing but a nuisance.

'I could go and find him,' said Cassandra, doubtfully.

'No!' said Livia. 'What happens if he comes back while you're gone? You wouldn't know. He's probably just waiting for the Pols to go away.' She clutched this thought to her, repeated it over and over in her head so there was no room for anything else.

Cassandra looked at her. 'Yeah, you're probably right.' She seemed different, thought Livia. Where was the confidence, the arrogance now?

'Why didn't the Pols bother to follow us down this street? They knew we came along here.'

'They're not interested, I told you. Too much like hard work to go chasing down narrow alleys like this. They're unfit. Probably gone into an entertainment centre instead.' Cassandra kept looking out of the grating. She chewed her lip.

Livia couldn't breathe. Where was Marcus? Had he been caught or shot? Was he trapped somewhere? Was he lost? Perhaps he had missed the turning? How would he ever find his way back? The relief of escaping with her life was replaced by a terrible fear for Marcus, which she now could not push away.

She sat down on the damp ground in the darkness. She felt suddenly weak. She was hungry but nauseous at the same time. She stank. She could feel wetness under her arms. Her head began to ache dully behind her eyes. And her ankle was throbbing. She felt it with her hand – it was tight inside her shoe.

They waited in the cold and dark. Cassandra stood, peering through the grating, the profile of her face dark against the light outside. She was chewing the inside of her cheek, unable to keep still. Livia listened to Tavius breathing heavily as he lay beside her.

She felt him shift closer to her. His shoulder touched hers and he left it there against her, needing her contact now.

Come back Marcus, please come back Marcus.

This is not like any other pain.

How did we think we could do this? How did anyone think we could? How could my parents ever think I could be a part of this? How could they have wanted me to be?

Come back, Marcus. Please please please please come back, Marcus.

When I hurt myself, it blocks out other pain. But now I can't make a pain that is worse than this. I don't even know how to start.

'He's coming!' shouted Cassandra and Livia's heart somersaulted. A huge grin spread across her face. She scrambled to her feet. 'Tav!' she said. 'Marcus is back!' and she felt her voice cracking as she said it.

A few seconds later she saw his legs come sliding

through the grating and she flung her arms around him. Cass slapped him on the back. Tavius, struggling to his feet, greeted him too. It was only afterwards, when they were walking back along the tunnel, that Livia realised: when she had hugged him, Marcus had felt cold and wooden. He had not returned her warmth. And he was silent, wrapped up. But they all were, she tried to reassure herself. They were all shaken by what had happened. And by what had so nearly happened.

She felt washed out, sluiced through by the up-and-down ride of raw emotion. Her mind was numb. She didn't know which feeling to feel.

None of them spoke as they walked back along the cold tunnels, led by Cassandra's torch. Only when they reached the door did Cassandra turn and say, 'No details. Leave it to me.'

They didn't have Lochinvar's oils with them. Livia was almost too tired to care, though she did find herself breathing through her nose as shallowly as she could.

The Outsiders watched them as they came through the hall. Livia was supporting Tavius, who was walking more and more slowly, his head hanging with weakness and pain and shock. The makeshift bandage was soaked with blood. Marcus was behind them. She couldn't see his face.

When they came to Cass's Place, Cassandra turned.

'You two, Marcus and Livia, go and wash, change if you want to. Livia, you've got blood on your clothes.' Her tone no longer seemed harsh and lecturing. 'I'll take Tav and get his arm seen to. There's someone who can fix it. I'll see you back here. And you know where food is, tea, whatever.' She took Tavius away.

Livia turned to Marcus. 'So, what happened back there? You had me worried!' she tried to say it lightly. How could she say what she had really felt?

'Nothing!' he snapped. 'Nothing at all, OK?'

'But ...'

'Get off my back!' he snapped. 'I'm going to shower.' And he walked off without looking at her. But she had seen his face. It looked twisted by something like fury. And it seemed to be directed at her. What had she done?

Did everything have to fall to pieces? What was left if everyone changed around her?

Weakly, she sat down. Looking round, she could see everyone busying about their tasks. Three men had just come back with two dead dogs strung on a pole and three bulging sacks. Rats, she guessed. The idea still horrified her. A woman nearby was gutting fish, expertly slitting their bellies and scraping the contents into a bucket. A group of children was listening quietly to a story. Milton wasn't there.

She knew they must all have seen her. But no one

came to speak to her. Not one of these people either knew or cared what they had just been through up on the streets. They were focused on survival.

Soon she could see Cassandra and Tavius approaching. Marcus was close behind. She avoided catching his eye. Still something shifted inside her when she saw him. Why was he shutting her out?

'You hungry?' asked Cassandra.

'Very.'

The four of them went over to the fire and Livia hung the kettle from the hook above it. They waited in silence for it to boil, passing round some biscuits. While they held the hot cups of tea in their hands, the silence swelled, until it was something they could almost touch. It was heavy. Oppressive.

Tavius spoke, his voice unsteady. His arm was tightly bandaged with a cloth the shade of wet sand. His face was drained of all colour, his lips grey and dry, his hair untidy. But his body was still now, no longer jerky. The effects of the drugs seemed to have worn off. He was almost back to normal, except without his old, careless half-smile.

'Look, guys, I know, it was all my fault. I can't believe I did that. Totally stupid. I'm sorry, OK?' He tried to smile properly but it was crumpled at the edges.

'We all did it, Tav,' said Livia. 'We all took funk.'

Tavius looked at her and tried to say something else. He didn't need to. She knew what he was feeling. They had been close to death that day. It was not easy to talk about.

She turned to Cassandra, forced herself to meet those perfect cool eyes. 'We all took that stuff. You told us not to and we just took no notice. It was my fault as much as anyone's. I'm sorry. Really sorry.'

Marcus said nothing. He swirled his tea, frowning.

'Yeah, OK,' said Cassandra. 'At least you know what's involved now.' She paused, thinking, and then spoke again, though not meeting Livia's eyes. 'And Livia, what you did, that was . . . pretty brave. Going back for Tav. He'd have been killed if you hadn't . . .'

Marcus stood up suddenly. He crashed his mug down on the table. Tea slopped out. He walked away without a word. The others looked at each other.

'What's got into him?' asked Cass.

'No idea,' said Livia. She wanted to go after Marcus. Wanted to shout at him, to tell him they were almost a team now, that the four of them could work together. But she was afraid of what he would say. There was an anger in him which she had never seen before.

Within a few minutes, he had come back. He sat down, stared for a moment at the ground and then spoke. 'Sorry. Forget it.'

'Sure,' said Cass. 'No problem.'

'No, actually, it is a problem,' said Livia, anger sharpening her voice. 'We all went through hell up there and what gives you the right to go all moody and furious and bloody rude? I want to know what's got into you.'

'Oh, you do, do you, Miss Perfect?' he spat back.

Now she wished she had kept quiet. This was spinning away from her. But she couldn't stop. Her anger grew like a sudden storm.

'Yes, Marcus, and actually I want to know why you didn't come back. We were worried sick and then you waltz along with no bloody explanation at all and treat us, me, as though I'd done something wrong. We thought you were DEAD, Marcus! What do you think that was like?' She forced her voice strong where it quavered at the edges. Her chest rose and fell, hard and fast. Her face felt hot.

There was a tiny pause. Then he spoke, no longer angry, but something else. Something more complicated. Colder. Worse. 'You want to know, do you? You really want to know what I was doing?'

'You bet I king do!' she replied, still too furious to stop.

'I was scared, if you want to know. Shit scared.' Now his voice rose fast. 'I saw the Pols. I saw Tav standing there. I saw you come back to get him. I saw the Pols see you. I knew they were going to shoot. And you know what I'd have done if this had been a story? If I was a storybook hero? I'd have acted, wouldn't I? I'd have done something to make them shoot at *me* and given you time to get away. That's what heroes do in stories, isn't it? But instead I hid, I king well hid, Liv! And I watched them shoot Tav, and nearly you, and you both could have been killed. And instead Tav was hurt, you were the hero and I was just a shitty little coward. And you know what? I always was a coward. You think I'm so cocky, never afraid, real risk-taker? It's all an act. Always has been. I am just a shitty coward.' His eyes glistened in the firelight. 'And that's why I didn't come back and that's why . . . that's why all this. This crap.' He ran his hands through his hair as though he would pull it out by the roots.

Livia didn't know what to say. Her anger was gone in an instant. She wanted to put her arms round him and tell him she didn't blame him. But he looked too fragile. The feeling that everything was careering out of control was overwhelming. If Marcus couldn't be strong, then what else could she rely on? He was right – she had thought he was brave. She needed him to be. She couldn't do this on her own.

Cassandra broke the silence. She seemed to take a

deep breath before she spoke. 'Don't blame yourself, Marcus. Any of you. It was my fault.' She stopped. Stared at the ground. They looked at her, surprised. She was chewing the edge of her thumb. Livia noticed that all her fingers were bitten, pink-edged, ugly. She had never noticed before.

Cassandra stood up, sat down again. Took another deep breath. And spoke. She didn't look at any of them. 'While we're all on the subject of feeling guilty, there's something I have to tell you. You aren't the only ones who are stupid, you know? You aren't the only ones who make mistakes. Dangerous mistakes.' They all stared at her. They had never seen her like this. Shaky.

'You remember I told you about my friend? The one who died? Well, it was my fault.' She paused. No one said anything. 'We were at Alex's flat. And I wanted some funk. Don't know why. I was bored. I didn't think it would do any harm – I'd had it a couple of times before. Will – that was his name – he didn't want any. Tried to stop me. But I took it anyway – I was irritated by how strong and damn perfect he was – and then I persuaded him to take some. I manipulated him. I even bribed him. I said . . . I said . . . Anyway, he did – take it. OK, I know he still could have said no but I just went on at him. God, I hated myself. I was just going ON! I was only doing it so I wouldn't feel guilty. He told me

I was like Eve, tempting Adam to disobey God. But, just like Adam, he did what I said. And then when we had to go, it was . . . it was just like Tavius today. He was out of control. We were near the canal and he went over and stood at the edge. He called to me. He said, "Cassie, come and look. Come and look at the sunset." And I did. You could see it between two moonscrapers.

'And then I saw the Pols. I saw them see us, both of us. And I ran. I ran before I shouted to him. Do you get that? I ran *before* I shouted! And when I reached the corner, I turned and I saw him crumple under the bullets, saw him twist and fall, towards the water. I saw his face scream at me without a sound and I saw the splash as he fell. And you know what the worst thing was, the thing I can't get rid of? I know what he was thinking as he fell.'

No one spoke. No one needed to. She was going to tell them anyway. 'He was wondering why I had run *before* I shouted. And even apart from that, if I hadn't made him take that stuff, he wouldn't have been so dopey anyway. He'd have known that you can't really expect to look at the sunset and get away with it in this shit-hole world. So now do you see why nothing any of you did today was halfway as bad as what I did?' And now she looked up at them, shiny-eyed, stared at them each in turn, as if challenging them.

'We're really sorry,' said Livia, 'about Will. Everything.' It sounded hollow and awkward, but she meant it. Now she could understand Cass's anger, her irritation with them, her disdain for them and why she shut herself off when they were taking the funk.

'Yeah, well, maybe you won't be so sympathetic when you hear the rest.'

They waited.

'Come on,' said Marcus. 'It can't be as bad as what I did.' He smiled slightly.

Cassandra looked at him. 'Actually, Marcus, it was exactly the same. When you were watching Tavius and not saying anything, hiding, too afraid to put yourself in the firing line, I was doing exactly the same. I was watching Livia. I saw her run towards Tavius, I saw her try to get him out of danger. Risking herself. And I did nothing. I stayed safe underground watching through the grating like some water-rat. All I could do was remember Will's face accusing me.'

Livia spoke. 'You don't know he was accusing you. You can't know what's in someone else's head. You are letting your own guilt and stuff just invent what seems to fit. Maybe he thought he'd put you in danger, staring at the sunset like that. He called you over, didn't he? You loved each other, didn't you?' Livia searched desperately to find some way out for Cass. There was something too awful about needing to speak to someone who was dead. To need to ask forgiveness but to know you can never have it.

'Yeah, we did, we did,' said Cass, rubbing her hands together as though trying to wash something off them. She brushed the back of one hand across her eyes. 'Well, I guess we all had a crap day, didn't we?'

'It wasn't the best, no,' agreed Tavius.

'I've known better,' said Marcus. And the spell was broken. They smiled at each other. Thin smiles, but with new understanding. Livia still wanted to say something to Marcus, to show him that she understood, to show him what she felt – but still she couldn't. Not yet. There was too much rawness. But they looked at each other and it was almost enough. For now.

'How about we all start again?' asked Cassandra. 'I've been a rubbish host. I'm sorry. Just, screwed-up stuff, you know?'

'Sure, said Livia. Hope rose in her. Maybe they really could do this. Maybe they could achieve something. Together.

'Hey,' said Marcus, 'it's like the *Three Musketeers*.'

'Except that there're four of us,' Cassandra pointed out.

'There were four musketeers in the *Three Musketeers*,' said Marcus. 'There *were* three and they were joined by d'Artagnan.'

'Well, that shows how much I know,' she said.

'One for all and all for one!' said Tavius. And they knocked their cups of tea together, slopping the warm liquid into the air.

They were bonded by invisible strands now. By what they knew about each other. Everything had changed between them, suddenly, dramatically.

Now Livia felt wrapped in warmth. It was like taking funk, but better. This was real. With funk, you entirely forgot the pain. But with real happiness, you remembered the pain, and that was what made it worth feeling. Funk was fake. It was all one colour. Bubble-gum pink. Funk was deadening, blunting, a place without tingling, without sparkle, sherbet without fizz. It was like kissing a beautiful statue.

Livia stood up. 'I'm going for a shower. See you later.' At the first step, pain knifed through her ankle and she winced, caught unawares.

'What's wrong?' asked Cassandra. And then she saw the swelling. 'When did you do that?'

'In that basement. It's nothing. I just landed badly.'

'You mean you did all that running, you ran back for Tavius, AFTER you'd done this?'

'I didn't really notice it. Too much else to think about. It hurts more now.'

'It needs to be strapped. And you should sit with it raised. After your shower, I'll strap it for you.'

'OK, thanks,' and Livia smiled at Cassandra. Their eyes met somewhere, catching each other's thoughts in new understanding. Nothing more needed to be said.

Later, gasping in the icy water of the shower, Livia shook away the fears of the day. It felt as though she had swum against a strong current and had reached the beach at the other side.

She managed to push aside the tiny nagging feeling, the knowledge, that soon she would have to face danger again. They would have to go to Center Tower.

5

Late into the evening, when they had eaten as much as they could manage of the crispy roasted dog, some fish fire-baked in its own oil, and potatoes cooked in the embers and smeared with butter and salt, they sat around the fire with the others. The four of them sat close together. Livia's foot was raised on a stool.

One man was missing. Was he one of the sick now?

Still no one else came to talk to them. Still Livia felt that she and Marcus and Tavius were unwelcome.

Cassandra frowned. 'There's something going on,' she whispered. 'Look over there.' Most of the other adults sat on the other side of the fire, huddled in one group, talking quietly together, every now and then looking over to the newcomers.

A small voice rose above the chatter and everyone became quiet. It was Milton. The groups on the other side of the fire listened to him, though they didn't look at him. Milton sat in his wheelchair, his back to the fire, the flames surrounding his thin hair in a golden light.

He began, his voice quiet but stronger now. They recognised the rhythm and the words – a curious mixture of stories they already knew, skilfully woven with his own story-telling.

'Listen! This is a tale of a world without end. It is a tale of weapons and of war. It is a story of love and of hate. You have heard many times of these deeds of good and evil. They are written in your hearts. I sing once again of strength and heroes. Of exiles, of outcasts, of suffering. I sing of passion, of strength, of truth. And now I pray for inspiration, to tell you once more how it all began. How a shadow was cast on our land and we were forced underground. It is hard to believe the gods in heaven could be so cruel.

'Once there was an ancient land, a place of green and plenty. This land had wealth and strength. But its inhabitants could not hold onto this beauty. They allowed their minds to be invaded. And destroyed.'

Everyone was still and silent as Milton spoke. He wove their history, their story. He told of the terrorist disasters and wars of the previous century. He told of how governments had used technology to protect the people. How the bubble cities had sprung up, eventually merging into one urban sprawl. How the choice was stark: enter our protected environment, and we will provide everything you need. Or stay outside, and receive nothing from us. Absolute safety, or constant danger and suffering. You choose. Follow our rules and we will care for you. Ignore our rules and we will care nothing for you. You will be Outsiders. You will have no rights.

Finally, he told of the beauty of the rebel Outsiders' lives. He told of their strength, their refusal and resistance. He painted their lives all the colours of passion and fire.

As he finished, Livia noticed that people were silent, most of them looking down.

Suddenly, a woman stood up. It was the hostile woman. Her cheeks leapt red with anger.

'Except it's not like that now, is it?' Her voice was brittle. Her eyes darted around, trying to gather everyone in her glare. But she would not meet the eyes of Cassandra and the visitors. 'These guests,' she almost hissed. 'They will destroy what we have. Soft nannied kids with no experience of suffering – what can they do? We don't need them. We will survive this virus – we always have. It strengthens us, as disease is supposed to do. It is natural. But this plan to change society, to infiltrate the Tower, it's foolish, dangerous, and it risks us all. What do you think the Pols will do when these children fail? They will flush us from our home like rats. Then there will truly be no hope. You have a dream, you always say,' she pointed at Milton, her finger stabbing the air. 'Your dreams are worse than any virus. Your dreams will destroy us all.' Her breathing was fast. She clenched her fists as tight as stones at her side.

Milton struggled to rise from his chair but Cassandra

gently held him back. He spoke. 'Helen, we have been over all this.'

'Maybe you have been over it enough, Milton, but I haven't finished. I have the right to speak, do I not? And I will speak. I will speak my mind.'

'Helen, we understand your pain. We know what you have been through.'

'Don't patronise me!' she yelled, her finger stabbing the air again. 'You know nothing, Milton. You have your precious daughter, do you not? What do you know? I will speak, now that these . . . these children are here, I will speak again.' She pushed her hair back from her eyes.

There was a murmuring of agreement amongst the Outsiders. Livia, Tavius and Marcus looked at each other. What undercurrents of tension were here?

A man stood up near Helen. He put his arms around her and tried to make her sit down.

Her voice softened towards him. 'No, Sol, I will speak. I need to speak. They should know that we don't support what they are here for.' The man let her go but stood beside her.

She turned back to face them all. Her eyes were fixed now on Cassandra.

'Right little bitch you turned out to be!' The hatred in her voice was shocking. Cassandra didn't move.

Tavius glanced at her, edged closer. Livia and Marcus looked at each other. Each shrank towards the other.

'Just whose side are you on, you little cow?' Helen continued.

'Helen!' said Milton, angrily. 'I will not have you talking to Cassandra like that. Whatever you feel, this is not right, not fair.' He began to cough.

'Oh, and just what is right and fair? I want to know why she has betrayed her promise to me! Look at her, sitting all so cosy with these strangers! She told me she didn't want them here either. You said that, didn't you?' she glared at Cassandra. Cassandra nodded, opened her mouth to speak, but Helen continued. 'So, why did you say that? Trying to get back into my good books, were you? Yes, well, after what you did, I wouldn't blame you.' She turned to Livia and the others. 'Did she tell you? Did she tell you what she did?' They looked at each other.

'Yes, I told them,' said Cassandra.

'Did you tell them properly?'

'Yes, I told them properly, Helen.' Cassandra stood up. She turned to Livia and the others. 'Will was Helen's son.' She looked back at Helen, who was standing now with tears in her eyes. 'I told them how I blamed myself. How I still do.'

'Yes, well, I blame you too. But you said afterwards

that you would be on my side in the so-called Great Debate. Didn't you? You said that you agreed with me, that you wanted just to leave everything alone, to let us carry on living like this, down here. To keep things as they were.' Livia saw a hurt look cross Milton's face.

Helen continued. 'So, what happened, Cassandra? Why the change of heart? Fallen for someone else, have you? Forgotten Will, have you?'

'No, I haven't and I never will forget him. But I've changed my mind. Freedom is not just about survival. If that's what we think, we're no better than the Citizens. Livia and Marcus and Tavius are here to help. They're going to carry on where Will left off and they will have to be as brave as he was. And you know what he wanted, don't you? Will wanted us to fight for our freedom, proper freedom. He wanted that more than anything. You know that. Don't you? Don't you?' she repeated when Helen did not at first reply.

'He was sixteen, Cassandra! What did he know?'

'I'm sixteen too and I know one thing! I know he would rather be dead than carry on just surviving like this. I know that now. The Pol laughed as he shot him, Helen, remember?'

'Don't!' shouted Helen. 'I don't want to remember his death!'

'He died to watch the sunset – you can't forget that!

And that's why we have to fight. And that's why I am glad Livia and the others came – because I now see why we have to fight to change things. Because the freedom to watch the sunset is worth fighting for.'

Helen looked around her. 'What about the rest of you? Plenty of you agreed with me before. Have you all changed your minds?' She turned to the man beside her. 'What about you, Sol – what do you think now?'

'I think the same as you, Helen, but what choice do we have? They will probably fail anyway and then we can just get back to the way we were.'

'That's if they haven't put us in danger!' shouted another man. 'What if the Governators decide we're a threat and order the Pols to hunt us out? It wouldn't take them long to find us if they wanted to.'

There were murmurs of agreement.

With a wheezing cough, Milton forced himself to his feet and stood by Cassandra.

'Call yourselves human?' he asked, his voice whispering and breathless now. 'Call yourselves better than animals! What great . . . achievement ever . . . came . . . by taking . . . the easy option? What was ever . . . achieved . . . without risk?' His face contorted. He bent forward and was racked with weak coughing. Cassandra put her arm around his shoulders, tried to make him sit down. But still he stood.

Pain creased his blind eyes. Livia sensed his power slipping away. No one looked at him. He could no longer speak through his rapid breaths.

She stood up, her ankle tight and throbbing. Her heart beat fast. She had not planned this and as she stood and saw everyone look at her, she felt her breath catch in her throat. She tried to make her voice sound strong.

'I am sorry . . . I have not spoken to you before. I am Livia. You . . . you never asked me who I was. And I am sorry you don't want us here.' She paused. Spoke more loudly. 'But look around you. Is this what you want? Is this a life?'

'It's the only one we have!' said Sol, angrily.

'But it isn't enough, is it? Stories, poems, songs, music, are they enough? This isn't freedom. This isn't the freedom our ancestors chose. You are slowly dying and there's nothing—'

'We'll survive this, I told you,' snapped Helen. 'We always do. We've had plagues, diseases before. We get through it. We survive. You don't know anything about it. You've had it easy.'

'Survival! It's not enough! What's the point of survival? You go from meal to meal, from day to day. You limp from one disaster to another, while above you the Citizens have everything you need. You are oppressed. The Pols can shoot you for their pleasure, exterminate you with a sneer – you are no better than rats to them. Is that what you want?' No one answered. Milton stared in her direction. Marcus, Tavius and Cassandra looked at each other.

She continued, more confident now. At last she had the chance to do something.

'You want to sit here and wait to die like rats? Fine, so we go back home and some of you survive this sickness and in fifteen, twenty years' time you'll have built up your numbers. Then what? Another disease? The Governators make some new rule? The Pols decide to come on a hunting trip, kill you all, shoot you like the dogs you eat? Or do you want to try to change your lives for ever, now? There's only one way to do that. You all know it. Center Tower. Someone has to go to Center Tower and find a way to attack the system from within. And it doesn't look to me as though there's anyone here apart from Cassandra who's prepared to do it.' She looked around. 'Well, is there? Do you want Cassandra to go on her own?' People looked at the ground. A few of them shook their heads.

Marcus stood up. 'Livia's right. There's no choice.'

'And just how do you think you're going to do it?' asked one man.

'I haven't the faintest idea how we are going to do it,' said Livia coolly, her voice calm but with something hard in her grey eyes. 'But I know that all we can do, all anyone can *ever* do, is our best. Choices, truth, free will – they're worth fighting for. We can't all sit and moan every time there's reason not to act. Some of us choose to act, to fight.'

'Hear hear!' said Milton, his face shining. 'The Poet couldn't have put it better himself.' He coughed again and wiped his hand across his forehead. He turned to the others around the fire. 'Well, do you hear her? Do you all agree? We let these young people try?'

Some muttered, some said nothing, but there were also a few noises of agreement. Livia spoke again. 'Think of our history, our stories, think of what our ancestors fought for in the past. Remember how hope always triumphed. Whatever disaster is thrown at humans, everything from the great flood to the invisible war, revolutions, massacres, plagues, genocide – they never destroyed hope. Only we can destroy hope. By giving it away. The choice is simple. We fight or we throw it all away. It's your choice.'

Some people looked at Helen. Her shoulders sank. She had given in. She turned to Sol and they sat down together.

The man with the lyre stood up. 'Bravely spoken,' he said. 'I, for one, wish you good luck. You'll need it.'

Another woman spoke. 'I think maybe, if anyone

can do it, you can. It takes a young person to tell us sometimes. What we don't want to hear. I wish you luck, too.'

Cassandra looked at Livia and smiled. Livia could hardly believe what she had done, how the words had come to her when she needed them. Marcus and Tavius looked at her in a new way, too.

More people nodded. A few called out their agreement. They looked more openly at Livia and the others. Now perhaps they seemed more curious than hostile, thought Livia. As people began to talk amongst themselves, and then slowly to disperse towards their beds, she saw Helen and Sol walking towards her.

Sol spoke. 'We still fear for the future, but we wish you luck as well. Don't we, Helen?'

Helen nodded, though she looked at the ground and bit her lip.

Sol spoke again. 'It's hard, you know. We have other children and we are afraid . . . I just hope you know how difficult it's going to be. And if you fail . . .' He shook his head. 'I am sorry. We wish you luck. Of course. Helen?'

Helen looked up, looked straight at Cassandra. 'Just don't forget . . .' but she didn't finish, only shook her head and walked away. Sol raised his hand to them with a sad smile as he followed her.

As everyone left, Milton spoke to Cassandra. 'Was Helen right?' he wheezed. 'Did you really agree with her? That we should leave things as they are?'

She looked down. 'Yeah, I did. After Will died, it all seemed so pointless. And I was scared.'

'And now? What do you really think?'

'I think we have to try. For freedom. Freedom to do more than survive. Livia was right.'

His thin face relaxed.

'We go to Center Tower as soon as possible,' said Cassandra. She looked at them all. 'Do we agree?'

They nodded.

A chill wrapped itself around Livia's heart. She pictured those moonscrapers with their black eyes. What dangers would wait for them in Center Tower? It was easy to speak brave words. But could she follow it through with action?

Part Five

Center Tower

This way for the sorrowful city.
This way for eternal suffering.
This way to join the lost people.
Abandon all hope, you who enter!
Inscription above the entrance
to Hell, in *Dante's Inferno*

1

It was four days before they began their journey. Four days, during which Tavius' arm healed and Livia's ankle strengthened till it was almost as good as new. It had been a long four days, spent waiting, planning, talking. And being afraid.

Now, more of the Outsiders were welcoming, taking opportunities to come and talk, to share food, tell them more about their lives. Livia and the others grew a new respect for them. This sickened existence was not the way it had been before. They had had a brave and passionate life, but years of disease and disaster had taken their toll.

The hall behind the curtain where the sick people lay and coughed and died was a constant reminder of what the three of them had left Balmoral for. Twice during the four days, someone else died, and the bodies, bedding and all their possessions were burnt to ashes.

Although each cremation took place deep in an unseen tunnel, there was also a ceremony in the hall. The music and the singing seemed exhausted and desperate, almost without power. It was as though they were all giving up.

Livia and the others kept their small bottles of oil with them like some sort of talisman. They shared the oil with the other Outsiders, too. The smell of lemon, tea-tree and orange became their shield, and if they could not smell it they felt vulnerable. Even Cassandra accepted the oil from them, though she seemed to do so out of friendship, not because she thought it would protect her from the disease.

'I've never been ill and I've never bothered with potions, so I'm not about to start now,' she boasted. 'This stuff at least smells nice, though — better than the usual stink.'

As the days passed, Livia became more afraid, uncertain again about whether she could do this, whether they could achieve anything in Center Tower. She didn't understand how the City could be as it was, and so she couldn't see a way to unravel it. Surely it was too much to ask? But there was no alternative.

Or, rather, there was an alternative. It was all around her.

The night before they left, she was unable to sleep. Eventually she gave up and went towards the main hall.

She intended to sit by the embers of the fire until she felt sleepy. But before she got there, she heard Milton's rasping breathing. She stopped at his shelter, looking through the slightly open door. He was asleep. She wished he was awake. She wanted to ask him about her parents. She wanted to know if they had said anything when they gave her to him. No one else would know apart from Milton. No one else would know whether it had hurt them.

I hope it hurt them. Not very nice, I know, but it would show they cared. I need to know. It would make them worth having as parents. Did they know I would be this frightened? Did they care? I wish they could know now.

And the only person who can tell me is asleep. It will have to wait till we come back.

And I want to ask him about all that stuff earlier – about everything being in the story? Surely, it means nothing, or nothing helpful. 'It lies there and becomes a part of you,' he said. So what? So much waffle.

Words, words, words. But what about action?

Stories are the past. What do they say about the future? Isn't that what's important? Aren't stories just something to listen to, something cosy, something comfortingly unreal? They don't really DO anything, do they? And isn't it what we DO that's important?

Later that night, as she lay on her mattress again and tried to sleep amidst the sound of snoring and whimpering, and rustling, the crackling of embers and the steady drip of water behind a wall, she had a sense of being on the edge of something. She could feel the rushing coldness of space in front of her. Something she could not see, and could only fear.

She wanted it and she did not want it.

This time, when she pressed her wrist against a sharp stone embedded in the floor, the pain was not enough. Like a weakening tide, it couldn't reach the rubbish to wash it away.

It's coming back again. The fear. What is it with me? Why one minute thinking I can do it, the next wanting to crawl away and hide? Wishing someone else could take the risk. Wanting it to be over. Why so changeable?

This is real fear, this dark cold thing that comes in the middle of the night when the world's asleep.

In the secret of the dark you can look inside yourself. When I spoke up that night, made that speech in front of everyone — it wasn't me. It was someone else.

And that stuff about being brave. When I saved Tav. I didn't feel so brave, if only they knew. I felt pretty bloody crap actually. Wanted to run. But something took over and it might have been bravery but it didn't feel the way I thought bravery

would feel: big and good and yellow and strong and lionlike.
Instead, it felt shitty and shaky and 'King well HURRY UP,
TAV!'

I'm going to have to do it again. And I don't know if I can.
I don't want to die. I don't want to die. Kill Tavius, kill
Cassandra, kill Marcus. Do it to them. Do it to them. Not
me.

Milton was right about one thing. It is in the story, isn't it?
In Nineteen Eighty-four, *when the so-called hero is faced*
with his greatest fear, he screams at his torturer in desperation,
'Do it to Julia! Do it to Julia!' Julia is the woman he loves.
And up till that moment, you had respected this hero. But now
you see that he's not as brave as you wanted him to be. It kind
of changes your perspective.

I always thought that was the saddest ending I ever heard.
Though it wasn't even the ending. The ending was even
sadder.

The next day, late in the evening, they set off. Milton
was lying in bed when they went to say goodbye to him,
his face sheeny with fever and exhaustion. His skin was
film-thin. Livia had had no chance to speak to him
during the day – he was always asleep, or had people
with him.

Cassandra put her hand on his forehead, brushing
stray hair from his face. His eyes opened.

'We're going now,' she said. We won't be back till the morning. Don't worry about us. We'll be careful.'

He squeezed her hand. 'I am proud of you,' he whispered. 'Proud of all of you.' His eyes drifted over each of them and he smiled. 'And I trust you.' Suddenly his eyes seemed to glaze and his eyeballs rolled up, flickering. His voice when he next spoke was distant and strange. Like another person speaking. And what he said was even more strange. It was as though he was reading from a book, or quoting from something.

'We are the dead. Our only true life is in the future. We shall take part in it as handfuls of dust and splinters of bone.' Then his face changed again, and his voice became his own, but harder and angry. 'No! Don't let it be! Not the saddest story in the whole universe! Don't let it happen!'

The four of them looked at each other. What was happening? He seemed delirious. Cassandra stroked his head. 'Hush, father, you're dreaming.'

Dreaming perhaps, but his words – about the handfuls of dust and splinters of bone – had sounded very familiar to Livia. She couldn't remember why. Some story perhaps.

His wheezing cough was the last sound they heard before leaving.

The Outsiders waved at them as they left, calling out

their good wishes. Even Helen raised her hand. As they left the hall and the door closed behind them, they knew that they were on their own.

Marcus and Cassandra led the way. Livia turned to Tavius. He looked at her and on an impulse she flung her arms around him. They held each other tight. She had never hugged Tavius before. Normally, he protected his space and you would not have thought of crossing it. Now, when it mattered, just in time, he was changing.

Perhaps I can do this now. Strong in myself and in my friends. We can do this.

I'll forget what I said last night. It was the sort of self-pitying stuff that comes in the hours of darkness when you are on your own. And in the morning you wonder how you could think it.

I may sound like two people, but that's how it is. I am two people, looking for the real one.

By this time tomorrow, we will all be back here safely. We must be. I can't think of a different ending.

And then I will ask Milton. I will ask him the only thing I will still need to know about myself.

Was I loved?

They were dressed for running and for the night. Dark leggings for the girls, looser trousers for the boys, and thick T-shirts. Springy shoes. Livia had plaited her hair out of the way and, as usual now, wore no make-up. It didn't seem important any more. They each carried knives. Livia, Tavius and Marcus had looked at the sheathed blades when Cassandra had put them in their hands. They said nothing as they fixed the weapons in loops in their belts.

The passages and tunnels, their dankness almost familiar now, passed in a blur. They came to the grating, and looked out at the silent street.

They climbed up and through the hole. A strange orange darkness glowed on the empty street. Round the corner, the bright lights of the crowded tubes and walkways snaked like filaments through the sky. If they looked up, they could see the night sky cloaking the city, but no stars. No stars anywhere, thought Livia. As though something thick and black blocked out space. She wished she could see the stars again. One more time.

Soon they were on the walkways and entering the glass tunnels, following Cassandra. They passed Citizens in every direction, all going to or from their entertainments. Laughter everywhere, lights, noise, music, glitzy screens, the neon stripes of flasers and slicing aquaoptic darts flashing across their vision.

They came to a place where many different walkways met. Multi-coloured signs pointed in all directions. Cassandra stopped and gave each of them a shiny blue coin. She met their eyes, as though to say, 'Concentrate – watch me.' She walked towards a barrier. A sign above it simply said GOVOZONE and, underneath, CENTER TOWER. Cassandra put her coin in a slot and the barrier slid sideways into nothing. She went through and the barrier slid back. The others did the same.

They found themselves in a brightly-lit hall with small orderly queues waiting at striped yellow and orange doors. They joined one of the queues and waited. Within a minute, they heard a gentle swishing sound and the doors opened. The queues moved forwards and they walked into the silver tube of a solatrain. A sweet smell of banana wafted across them. A moment of dizziness, a slightly drugged smilingness. Cassandra looked at them with a tiny warning in her eyes. Livia remembered her telling them that the solatrains pumped a calming aroma into the air. Not funk, but something simply pleasant.

They sat down and, copying everyone else, belted harnesses around themselves. The doors slid closed and, within seconds, the tube shot backwards at immense speed. They tried not to look surprised. They needn't have worried. No one was looking.

Livia felt Marcus nudge her. She saw where he was looking. Pols, three, black-shaded eyes. Her heart rate immediately increased. She looked away. Tavius had noticed too. So had Cassandra. They kept their eyes fixed straight ahead. Expressions blanked. One of the Pols was flicking a catch on his bodysuit. Flick. Flick. Flick. But none of them looked at the four Outsiders. None of them seemed interested in anything. They didn't even look at their scanners.

Livia was aware of moving at huge speed, though there were no windows so she could see nothing outside the tube. Every now and then, there was the sensation of turning to one side or another. Soon, after perhaps five minutes, the vehicle slid to a halt and the doors hissed open. They followed Cassandra again. It was almost lulling not to have to think, just to follow.

Outside, in the glass tunnel with its moving walkway, there were fewer people now. No Pols for the moment. Everywhere they could see polyglass, silver, micro-alloy, plastic, squishtic, harsh white light and the brilliant clarity of signs projected into the air through streams of aquaoptics. Everything smooth. Everything clean. Soon, Cassandra veered sharply to the right and they found themselves going downwards, towards street level.

Once on the street, there was the orange darkness again, thick above them. They shivered despite the warmth. They were in a place of few people, and little need for the usual bright lighting. They seemed to be at the back of buildings, their walls black and sheer. Men and women dressed in white overalls and gloves unloaded boxes from solavans and tossed them into delivery chutes. They didn't notice or care about four strangers. There was an air of conveyor-belt boredom.

Cassandra turned down a narrow alley and began to hurry. She didn't need to look back. She knew the others would follow. Now the darkness was more intense. Livia felt that detachment again, not knowing where she was, a dizzying feeling. Another alley, and another. Each one darker, narrower than the one before. The occasional nearby shout or clatter. And always the distant faint jangle of music.

Suddenly, at a corner, Cassandra stopped. They gathered around, breathing hard. 'Along there,' she whispered. 'It's one of the back entrances. And if you look up now . . .'

They craned their necks backwards. At first Livia saw nothing. Then she realised that it was the nothing that she was meant to be looking at. A sheer black wall rose so far into the sky that it was endless, stretching for ever into the void.

'Wow!' breathed Tavius. It was the only thing to say.

'This is it,' said Cassandra. 'Good luck, everybody.' They knew what they had to do. They had planned it over the last few days. Cassandra and Will had spent many hours investigating the back entrances to Center Tower and they believed they had discovered a way in. Now they could only hope it would go according to plan.

Livia strained every sense to detect the approach of danger. She could see the blank-walled back of the Tower beside her. No windows, no lights. Like a giant with his back turned. Like playing grandmother's footsteps with a monster so huge it could block out the stars.

'Let's go!' whispered Cassandra. They ran together to a goods entrance. Slid round the corner and found themselves going steeply downwards, underneath the building. It was the entrance for delivery vans.

'Where are they?' whispered Tavius. They were looking for the delivery lifts, the complex system of narrow shafts where provisions were delivered into wire mesh baskets to take each item to the right floor of the building. There were other shafts for items to be brought down, all with mesh baskets fixed at intervals along each thin metal wire. The wires were continuous, so that when each basket reached the top it could come back down a different shaft.

'Over there!' said Cassandra and they all ran to an opening in the wall. Inside was a narrow passage with a row of black holes showing the entrances to the shafts. Easy! They were not expecting security at this stage – no Citizen would ever dream of breaking into Center Tower. Why bother?

One by one they climbed into the first opening, squeezing past a wire basket waiting at the bottom. They had discussed travelling up in the basket, pressing the button once they were in, but it was too risky. It was impossible to know if someone would be there when it stopped. They might walk into the arms of the Pols, whose headquarters were in Center Tower.

Instead, as planned, they found the service ladder that went up each shaft beside the baskets. The lift shaft was square, between one and two metres wide. Each basket was open on one side, containing ropes to secure packages. The ladder was on the side next to the basket's opening, with just enough room to squeeze past the basket if they squashed themselves very flat.

They climbed the ladder in silence. Cassandra went first, followed by Tavius, Livia and then Marcus. Once they had passed the dangling basket, there was more room. A minute later they came to the next basket and had to squeeze past again. Livia began to sweat. The chute was airless and thick with the smell of old plastic and metal. They were in near darkness, only a dim grey glow from somewhere high above them and occasional ventilation gaps in the wall beside the ladder. It was like climbing a chimney.

Livia tried to move her arms and legs in a rhythm, searching for the hand and foot-holds by instinct. Suddenly her hand felt air and she panicked. She flailed her fingers, desperately searching for the rung. Marcus stopped behind her, saying nothing, but she could feel his tension. She resumed the rhythm, her heart pounding.

Her arms and legs began to tire. It became harder to take each step. She could hear the others breathing loudly. How far could they go like this? Stop thinking about how far and just do it, she told herself. This is only the beginning.

Each time they came to another wire basket, the rhythm was broken and they had to squeeze tightly past again.

Tavius whispered from above her. 'Stop, guys. Cass has come to a floor level. When we get there, we've got to get across the lift shaft. Tell Marcus.' She hissed the message back to Marcus. She could hear Cassandra and Tavius above her, but couldn't see what they were doing. A few more steps and she could just make out their shapes over to the right. On the other side of the shaft.

'Over here!' they called. 'Jump!'

She was just about to jump, was just taking a breath before leaping the short distance to the ledge, when a loud metal grinding noise rose from all around them. The lift was moving. 'Watch out!' shouted Marcus from below. She squashed herself as tightly as she could against the wall, heard a yell of pain from Marcus, and held her breath as the wire basket rushed past. And another. And another.

It was probably less than half a minute before the screeching of metal stopped and everything was still. She was unhurt. What about Marcus? 'Jump, quick!' said Cassandra. Livia jumped and was grabbed by the others. Marcus' head appeared, slowly. He didn't seem to be using his arm properly. When he reached them, he paused, braced himself and jumped.

'You OK?' asked Livia.

'Smashed my shoulder against that basket thing. It's OK.' She could see him smile in the dim blue light that came from the doorway. 'You can always kiss it better, if you want, Liv.' He swung it to lessen the pain.

'Maybe later,' she said, holding the smile secretly inside herself.

They were standing in the opening to a room. They moved cautiously into it. Blue exit signs glowed dimly in the gloom. No people.

'Where are we?' asked Livia.

'I've no idea,' replied Cass. 'But we've climbed far enough. Time for the next stage.' They all knew what this meant. The next stage was to get into the main part of the building and use the proper lifts. It would be impossible to reach the top of the building by climbing up the ladder. There were well over two hundred floors. Besides, they couldn't be absolutely sure that it was the very top floor they wanted. That was what everyone said but they couldn't know if it was just a myth.

'This room seems dead enough. It's obviously closed down for the night. I reckon we're safe here for now,' said Tavius.

'We're inside! I can't believe we're inside!' said Marcus. Livia was looking around. The room was vast, stretching into darkness far in front of them. It contained rows and rows of shelves. She looked more closely. Books.

At first this seemed so normal to her that she didn't understand the significance. All the familiar books from her childhood. All the well-known stories which formed the rhythm of their lives. She recognised the spines and titles, the authors. There were books she had hated and others she had loved. Some she had understood, others that had not touched her.

But why were they here? In Center Tower, the

centre of government of a state which despised stories and poetry?

'What's going on?' asked Marcus. 'Every piece of literature in a country where no one will ever read it?'

'Not every piece,' said Cassandra slowly, scanning the rows. 'There's nothing in any language apart from English.'

'So? That's hardly surprising. No one speaks any other language any more.' Tavius picked one out carefully and blew the dust from it. It crackled with age and the spine disintegrated as he opened it.

But Cassandra shook her head, as if thinking.

Livia was silent. Although she had been frustrated by Milton's confusing message about everything being 'in the story', his words had stayed with her. Was this a clue? Here were all the stories. But what did they have to do with anything? And this room, it felt unused. Dust coated everything. A couple of chairs lay on their sides. There was one computer, but it looked old.

Marcus sat down in front of it. Grime clung thick on its screen and on the table. He touched a switch at one side. Nothing happened. It was dead.

'What's it all for?' he wondered aloud.

'Perhaps some people here want to read,' suggested Tavius. 'Perhaps we are wrong to think none of them read.'

'But stories are banned,' said Marcus. 'We know that. Stories are drummed out of them from birth. They just don't exist as far as the Citizens are concerned.'

'Look, we're getting nowhere,' said Cassandra, looking at her watch. 'We'll run out of time before we've done anything at this rate.'

'OK. We ready?' asked Marcus. 'Good luck everyone.' Livia felt his hand take hers. She squeezed his fingers. He smiled at her and she smiled back. She wanted him to . . . but it was too late. Their fingers parted and she could still feel his touch on her skin.

They went towards the door. When Cassandra passed a hand over the small screen to one side, the door opened. Leaving a room was not a problem. Entering would be more difficult. Some doors would require identification. They had none.

Nervously, they left the safety of the room with all its books. They needed to find the lifts. It was rumoured amongst the Outsiders that security in Center Tower was as patchy as everywhere else – the Governators and Pols had had so many decades of no one bothering to commit crime that most security systems were weak. Any crime that might be committed tended to be at street level, by a degenerate Outsider or a Citizen who had taken the wrong amount of funk or made a mistake with his pim scrip – problems that were quickly detected and dealt with by the medi-services. No one ever expected Center Tower to be infiltrated and it was this element of surprise that Cassandra and the others were relying on.

On the other hand, if they were caught – what then? Livia remembered those tiny gleaming guns with a shudder. She wished it was all over. For a moment she wished she could hide somewhere. But she pushed the thought away. They had to do this, even though the fear was something that squeezed the air from her lungs.

They listened carefully, before moving out into the passageway. The door closed behind them. 'Language Center,' said a sign above it.

The corridor was empty in both directions. To one end was a mirrored bubble lift. They moved quickly towards it. The doors opened. They didn't enter. Too risky. Anyone might be at the other end.

A sign outside the lift showed a long list of department names. They were on Floor 2. At the very top of the list was 'Control Center'. Then Livia noticed the number of the top floor. Although there were 249 floors numbered before it, the number of the top floor was 101.

2

Floor 101. The meaning of that number was branded into her memory. The number of the torture room in *Nineteen Eighty-four*. The room where you meet your worst fear and where the hero betrays his friend and lover. The saddest story she had ever read.

Where had she heard that before? The saddest story . . . And then she remembered. It was what Milton had said before they left. 'Not the saddest story in the whole universe! Don't let it happen!' But what did it mean? It was like seeing a few pieces of a jigsaw – you can see they belong in the same picture but you can't see what the picture is.

There wasn't time to talk to the others. A tinny voice spoke from the lift. 'Enter, please. Going up.'

Marcus pointed into the lift. 'Look, it's one-way glass. If we get in, we can see out but no one can see in.' Just then they heard footsteps. Voices.

'Quick! In!' urged Marcus. There was no choice. They jumped in and the doors closed with agonising slowness as two Pols came round the corner. Cassandra keyed 101 into the touchpad.

A soft woman's voice spoke from the wall. 'You have not requested clearance. Please place your finger on the panel below.' Cassandra did. The voice said, 'You do not have Code Red clearance.' Livia kept her hand on the door-close panel. Her hands were sweaty, the muscles in her face tight. Her heart felt as if it was thumping in her throat. Hurry! Hurry! What if the Pols wanted to come in? Through the wall, she could see them walking slowly towards the lift, looking straight at it. It felt as though they were looking straight at her. They can't see me, she kept reminding herself. They can't see me.

'Floor 235!' said Tavius. 'Look – it's the highest we can go.' He pointed to a sign which reminded personnel that above floor 235 they needed Code Red clearance. Marcus jabbed the number 235 onto the touchpad and the lift began to move rapidly upwards. Every two or three seconds they passed another floor. Through the walls of the lift, they could see rows of empty desks and dim blue lights, on one floor a restaurant, on another a gymnasium, eerily empty as the workers had gone home for the night. On several floors they saw a chilling sight: dozens of Pols, relaxing, playing games, lounging in front of screens. The Pol headquarters.

'Shit!' said Cassandra. At first Livia thought it was because she had seen the Pols but she was pointing towards the screen. The number 220 had lit up. Someone was going to get in at floor 220! The lift was now at 214. Livia smashed her fingers onto the touchpad, pressing 215. Too late – the lift was already at 216. Her brain spinning, she pressed 219 and a few seconds later the lift hissed to a halt. The doors opened.

Not knowing what would be outside, they ran. Another corridor. Empty. No! Voices! Coming from that corner. They raced the other way. Round a corner. Voices again. And footsteps. From both directions. A door. Tavius pressed his finger over the entry panel. The door didn't open. A red light flashed above it. Code Red.

They ran further. Another door. The same. Locked. The Code Red light flashing.

The voices were nearer. Just round the corner.

Another door in front of them. The red light again. Marcus noticed a gap at the edge of the door. He put his fingers through and pulled it sideways. It moved slowly. Too slowly. Livia slipped her fingers in and they pulled together. The door wheezed open with a broken grating noise. They rushed in. Cassandra passed her hand over the panel on the inside and the door slid shut.

It was a changing room. Rows of metallic blue lockers. Shower cubicles to one side. Clothes on the floor, some black Pol bodysuits hanging on hooks. Boots lying scattered. Their eyes scanned rapidly, trying to take in everything in front of them, trying to find a place to hide.

Voices outside the door. They looked at each other. No time to lose. They ran round the end of the lockers, and hid out of sight of the door. They were each behind a different row of lockers, pressed against the cold sides. Livia was nearest to the door. Marcus was the closest to Livia. They fixed their eyes on each other while straining every sense to catch any noise. She stared at every part of his face, as if she might never see him again. His hair was tangled. His eyes were steely. A shadow lay on his jaw. There was blood on his T-shirt at the shoulder. How did he not look frightened, she wondered?

They heard the swish of the door open. Voices, louder. Men, probably two.

'Kay, see ya after my shower. Be 'bout twenty minutes, is all.'

'Sure, see ya.' And the voices stopped as the door closed again and they heard the footsteps of one person cross the floor. The sigh of a zip. A grunt. The swish of a shower. The click of a locker door opening, a shadow moving, clothes rustling, a small gasp and then sudden silence. No movement now. No rustling. Livia could hear her heartbeat, tried desperately to keep her breathing to nearly nothing. Surely he would hear her?

And then she looked down and saw a shadow underneath the lockers, moving across the floor. Slowly. The man was walking towards her. He knew someone was there. If he walked round the corner he would see all of them. Did he have a gun in his hand? Surely he did. He could kill them all before they could do anything.

Suddenly, she knew what she had to do. She looked at Marcus and their eyes met. No, yelled his eyes. Yes, hers replied. She silenced him with her stare. Then, not knowing what would happen, not knowing what she planned but knowing she must act, and not looking back at Marcus, she stepped out slowly and smoothly from her hiding-place.

3

Livia was not prepared for how the Pol would look close-up or for her sickening fear as he saw her. The rubber top of his black bodysuit was pulled off his head, hanging down his back like a dead snakeskin. His neck was white and thick with surplus fat. A few hairs curled from the top of his bodysuit.

He held his gun in front of him, pointing at her throat, as he took in the fact that she was just a girl. Then he began to smile.

Slowly, her hands in front of her to show they were empty, she moved slightly to one side and round, away from the lockers. He turned a little, to keep her in front of him. If she could move further round, he would soon have his back towards the ends of the lockers, where the others were. She hoped Marcus would not do something until he was completely behind the man.

She had no plan. She was playing for time. She just knew that the choice had been simple: stay where she was and face death for all of them, or come out and face him herself, maybe buy some time, maybe talk to him, anything. Wasn't that how it happened in stories? That the heroes escape from certain death through some last-minute miracle?

Now, with her heartbeat high in her chest, trapping her breath, and the man walking slowly towards her, she didn't know if she could face this. It didn't feel like a story.

He was coming closer, staring at her, a soft smile smirking over one side of his mouth. His lips were parted, a sheen of spittle on them. His gaze moved downwards. His tongue slid out. It licked his top lip slowly. She tried to move a little more to the side. His back was not yet completely towards the end of the lockers. If the others tried to attack him now, the man would see them first. He would shoot at least one of them. Perhaps her.

She smiled at him. Her breathing was fast. Her heart beat so loudly she thought it must burst. Imperceptibly, she slid slightly further round. He took a step towards her. Now she could smell his breath. His shaven head, stubbled in grey, shone with a new sweat. He stood, his feet wide, his legs and body and arms encased in black, now so close that he could have touched her.

Slowly, invisibly, she moved round a little more. Now he almost had his back to where Marcus and the others were hiding. She thought she saw a shadow move. Not yet! she willed her thoughts to Marcus. She forced herself not to look, to keep her eyes fixed on the man's. She must trap his attention.

Her legs were shaking, jellied and weak, turning to water. She must stay standing.

'So?' said the man, his voice smooth. 'Want it then, do you?' The tip of his tongue slid out again. She said nothing but her skin crawled. He raised his gun and moved it towards her face. With the tip of the thin barrel, he softly stroked the side of her cheek. She met his gaze. Something cruel crossed his eyes.

'You should be scared, girl. You should be scared of me? You shouldn't be in here, shouldn't you? Two cleaning staff in the male changing-room, remember, girl? For your safety. What will I do with you? I should tell your supervisor, should I? How'd you like me to tell your supervisor? Could get you a punishment, could this. Mebbe there's another way, but?' The gun barrel traced its way down the side of her neck and across to her throat. It stopped. Her breathing quickened. Black dizziness swam across her eyes. She began to lose control, felt herself swaying.

In her horror, she felt the man's hand at her waist, felt it worm its way underneath her T-shirt and up against her skin, slowly moving upwards. She wanted to scream, to run. She was paralysed by his foul fingers crawling up her body and the gun at her throat. But she must not scream, must let this happen, must wait until . . .

. . . the moment shattered. Through splintered eyes she watched as though from a distance. Marcus and Tavius leapt forward, each grabbing one of the man's arms. The gun span across the floor. A huge red gash split the man's throat and blood shot into the air and splashed her face as his eyes rolled upwards in sudden death. He fell, his head cracking on the floor, and Cassandra knelt above him, her clean knife pointing at him in case he was not yet dead. Blood was slowly pooling on the floor under his neck.

Livia's knees buckled and she collapsed, gasping. Someone caught her as she fell. It was Marcus, blood-stained knife still in his hand. She retched as she wiped the man's blood from her cheek.

'It's OK. You're OK, Liv,' he whispered. His eyes blazed with fury as he held her tight. Her body kept shaking, and each time she thought of the man's leering smile and remembered his sweet breath and wet lips, and that horrible crawling hand, she shuddered.

'We have to get moving,' urged Cassandra, looking at Livia. 'I'm really sorry, Liv, but we have to hurry.'

'Come on, Liv,' said Marcus, brushing her blood-wet hair from her eyes. She took a deep breath. There was no time for this, no time to think or choose. Steadying herself, she focused on what had to be done. Forced herself not to see in her head the memory of that gaping throat. Pushed her horror away to a place where it didn't matter.

Tavius smiled at her. 'OK?'

'Sure. Never better,' she said, through a clenched jaw. And icy fingers crawled over the skin of her back, like a ghost's breath.

They hurried to hide the body. Several lockers were open and empty and with difficulty they stuffed the man into one. The limbs were dead weights, cold and floppy. The four of them avoided each other's eyes. A man was dead, his throat slit. That was not easy to think about. His blood was on all of them. Now they had stepped in so far that they had passed the point of no return.

Using towels and water from the showers, they hurried to clean up the blood, ears tuned to any noise outside. Twice footsteps approached, and voices, and each time they froze. Each time the voices passed.

Livia used water from the shower to remove most of the blood from her face and hair. She could smell it. She didn't think she would ever wash all the blood away.

Yet, at the same time, she was glad the man was dead.

They scrambled into four of the black bodysuits that hung from hooks, pulling them over their own clothes. Fumbling with the zips, they frantically fastened themselves in, tugging the skin-tight hoods over their heads. They kicked off their own shoes and put them in the rubbish chute, pulling on boots they found lying around. There were no guns, only empty holsters.

No, there was one gun – on the floor where the man had dropped it. They all looked at it. 'Give it to Livia,' said Cassandra. 'She deserves it.' Livia took it, and held it in her palm for a moment. It weighed almost nothing. Quite different from the guns she was used to using at Balmoral. She slipped it into its holster under her arm. She knew she would use it if she had to. Blood will have blood, they say.

Black sunglasses hung from hooks. They put some on. Oddly, the light still seemed the same – they were only for effect. The difference between them and the Pols now was that they were not wearing the tiny earpieces that transmitted instructions. With luck, no one would notice.

Dressed in evil, they began to feel strong.

They walked towards the door.

'Wait,' said Cassandra. 'We have a problem.' The others looked at her. 'This Code Red,' she said. 'The entry panels on the doors are fingerprint panels. Probably don't use eye-rec systems because of the sunglasses.'

'And we don't have the right fingerprints,' said Marcus. None of them said what they were all thinking. After a pause, Tavius spoke, his voice hard.

'I'll do it.' He took his knife and opened the locker door where they had stuffed the man's body. The other three didn't look at each other while he did it.

Through hazy thoughts, Livia saw that Tavius had changed. Perhaps they all had. Perhaps you just did what you had to do when the time came.

See what we can do when we need to? It's not so hard when you don't think too much. It's one step at a time. It's life or death. We've killed a man, slit his throat. Why would we cringe at the thought of cutting off a dead man's finger?

They were ready to go. Listening carefully, hearing nothing, they nodded at each other. Marcus met Livia's eyes. 'It's OK,' she said to him quietly. 'I'm OK.'

Cassandra passed her hand over the door panel and it swished open. The corridor was empty. Quickly, they walked out. Towards the lift. The lift doors opened and they walked in. The doors closed and they were safe. For a while.

'So? Floor 101?' asked Marcus.

They all nodded.

4

When Tavius pressed the dead man's finger on the ID panel and input the number 101, Livia found she could watch without feeling anything. She was numb. The fear had gone somewhere else.

If she had ever imagined this, knowing that death could be round the corner, seeing a man die in front of her, she would have visualised being paralysed with fear, desperate to wake from the nightmare. But she was not.

Nothing is as bad as imagining.

On their way up the thirty-one floors, they saw nothing but darkness outside the lift. No lights shone there. They had no time to wonder why.

The lift whispered to a halt and the number 101 flashed. The doors opened and they walked out. The corridor was empty. It was more than empty. It was heavy with emptiness. The air was strange, as though it had not been disturbed for a long time.

Everything seemed to glow with a faint green light. It seemed to come from everywhere, the walls, the ceiling, the floor.

They walked along the corridor, their footsteps silent in soft-soled boots. Round the corner, nothing. Another corridor. The green light stronger now. No doors, no rooms, only the glowing walls. No pictures, no lights, no gratings, no buttons, no cameras.

Far in front of them they could see the corridor become wider, opening out. As they approached, they could see around the corner a huge room. Soon they were in it, although there had been no doorway to walk through.

The room was full of people. People sitting at computer screens. People relaxing in chairs. No one looked up.

The four of them walked as confidently as possible into the room. They didn't want to draw attention to themselves. Still no one looked up. There was a background chattering noise. But when they looked more closely, they couldn't see anyone speaking. There was quiet music but where did it come from? Livia noticed that in fact if she listened carefully she could hear several types of music all at once. She could smell peppermint, but sweeter. Then she thought it was banana, then roses, then almonds.

Still no one looked up. In amazement, Livia saw Cassandra march firmly up to a man sitting at a screen and touch him on the shoulder. Her hand went through him. Cassandra turned to the others. 'Holograms!' she whispered. 'They're all holograms.'

Tavius touched one of them. When his hand went

straight through, his mouth opened in disbelief.

Cassandra pushed back her sunshades and pulled the black hood away from her head. The others did the same. Livia ran her hands through her hair. She felt greasy, sweaty. She hadn't worn make-up for days. Tav's hair was plastered to his forehead and he didn't even bother to do anything to it, she noticed.

At the far end of the room was a screen, stretching high towards the ceiling, dome-shaped at the top. It looked as though it should be transparent but it wasn't. The green light seemed to come from behind it.

They walked towards it and round the screen.

There sat a man. A little old man with a bald head and a wrinkled face. He was staring at a huge computer screen suspended in the air by nothing. Across it flashed words too fast to read.

The man swivelled towards them. A white cat sat on his lap and he stroked it. One of his eyes was milky and glassy. The other a piercing blue.

He spoke. 'What a surprise! Although I suppose it shouldn't be a surprise. I should have known. In the circumstances.'

'Who are you?' asked Livia.

'Why! I hardly know myself! At least, I know who I was when I got up this morning but I think I must have changed several times since then!'

Not someone else who spoke in riddles, thought Livia. But his words sounded familiar. Something from a story again. Without warning and without knowing why, she smelt the Poet. The memories came rushing back. Stories. Rhythms. Patterns.

Suddenly, oddly, the man began to cry. Two tears trickled down the sides of his nose. A word flashed into Livia's mind: 'gin-scented'. His tears were gin-scented. How did she know? She had never smelt gin and, besides, she wasn't close enough to his tears. Yet she could smell them as though they were falling from her own eyes. Then, just as suddenly, the tears stopped. 'You want to know my name?' he asked.

'Yes,' they said.

'Call me Ishmael,' he grinned. And then Livia knew. It wasn't just the way the dust motes shone in the light in front of his face. It was what he said. She passed her hand across his eyes and part of him vanished into nothing, then reappeared when she took her hand away.

'Not real. A hologram. And he's speaking from stories,' she said to the others. 'I don't know why yet. This green light everywhere – it's the Emerald City – you know, *The Wizard of Oz*. In that story they find everything controlled by "a little old man with a bald head and a wrinkled face". "Call me Ishmael" – everyone knows that – the opening of *Moby Dick*. And

the stuff about hardly knowing who he was himself –
that's *Alice Through the Looking Glass*. The tears – "Two
gin-scented tears trickled down the side of his nose." It's
straight from *Nineteen Eighty-four*. What else have we
missed?'

'And that's why this is Floor 101,' said Cassandra.
'*Nineteen Eighty-four* again – the room where your worst
fear is.'

'And?' asked the man, smiling again now. 'What IS
your worst fear?'

'If he's a hologram, how come he can talk to us?'
asked Tavius. 'The other ones out there didn't do that.'

'It's the computer talking to us,' said Marcus. 'If you
stand here you can tell the voice comes from the
computer. The computer is creating the hologram.'

'You talk to it, Cass – you know the technology
better,' said Tavius.

Cassandra sat down in the chair, where the hologram
was. As it disappeared, the flashing words on the screen
vanished and the man's face appeared there instead. He
spoke.

'Good evening again. How delightful to meet you.
Real humans! Not like those dull holograms out there –
I know I created them for my own amusement but it's
not the same. It must be . . . oh, I don't know – years
and years since I spoke to a human. Now I can have a

real conversation. Now we can really rock. Would you like that?'

'Yes,' said Cassandra.

'Password, then, please. If you would be so kind. Oh! I am enjoying this!'

'Aren't passwords a bit old-fashioned? We have Code Red clearance.'

'Of course you have Code Red clearance. You wouldn't be here otherwise. But I am quite elderly and somewhat traditional and I do still like passwords. The thing is that the very last time a human came here, the last time a human had any sort of control at all, he set a password. And then, of course, he, er, disappeared. Mysterious circumstances, as they say. I always wondered if a computer killed him with a poisoned pim scrip. Surely not! A computer? But the problem for you is that without the password you can do no more than chitchat with me. You can't actually DO anything. Whereas, with the password, of course, you could. If you had the password you would have control. Again.'

'I've forgotten the password.'

'I want the password.'

Cassandra looked at the others. 'What the hell do we do now? Ideas?'

What was the point of guessing? Out of the thousands of words in the English language, not to mention countless names and infinite possibilities of invented words, how could they possibly guess?

The man on the screen spoke again.

'I am waiting.'

'Can I ask you some questions first?'

'Ooh, a game! Like twenty questions, you mean? I am good at games.'

'Yes, like twenty questions.'

'Certainly, but I don't think you'll have time for twenty. You'll have to hurry. You don't know how soon those nasty Pols will realise what's happening. They're not allowed up here – until I order them. I could summon them now, of course, but I think I'm enjoying myself too much. For the moment. A question, please!'

'Are you real?'

'What's real? You're talking to me, aren't you? I think. Therefore I am.'

'But you aren't human.'

'That's not a question. Besides, how do you know? I talk like a human, don't I? I know more than a human. I can compute a billion calculations in a fraction of a second. I can search the entire works of literature and find . . .'

'Do you feel?'

The face went blue. 'I'm feeling blue! Can't you tell?'

'What am I feeling?'

'What do I care? If I call the Pols, you will be feeling fear. I think I will call the Pols. I FEEL I will. I am just itching to do it. So, you will have to find the password. If you do, you will be able to stop me. If you don't, you won't. I'm bored with twenty questions. This is the new game.'

'What about a clue? Computers always used to give a clue if someone forgot the password.'

'What is my name? That's the clue. Guess my name.'

'That's not a proper clue. That's just repeating the question. A proper clue, or you aren't playing by the rules,' said Cassandra.

The face frowned. 'Certainly, I would always want to play by the rules. Here is the clue: if you don't guess my name, the baby gets it. Or, more accurately, you don't get the baby. And now, the clock is ticking. If you don't guess my name before the time runs out, I call the Pols. Fair?'

They looked at each other. The man stared out of the screen. His eyes became twin clocks, counting down the seconds. Fifty-three seconds to go.

'Stories, literature – think of all the names you can,' urged Marcus.

'Shakespeare? Dickens? Austen? Huxley? Thackeray?' said Tavius. He continued to list all the names he could think of.

'Or characters,' said Livia, her thoughts spinning. They shouted out the names of the characters from all the stories they could think of. It was hopeless, ridiculous. They would never get there like this.

The man looked impassive. His fingers drummed on the surface in front of him.

Forty seconds to go.

'What do you mean, you don't get the baby?' said Cassandra.

'Exactly what I say. That's the clue.'

Livia's mind span. She thought of the people who were relying on them. Could they fail so soon? The baby gets it. Or, you don't get the baby. What could it mean? And yet the meaning was out there. She could almost . . . No, it flicked away.

Thirty seconds to go.

She thought of her parents, of the Outsiders who had not trusted them, how she had persuaded them that they should. She thought of their friends, up in Balmoral, waiting for them to succeed. Even their teachers. She pictured Milton, his ashen face gasping out words of encouragement. He had said he trusted them. The Poet.

Twenty seconds to go. Still the others rattled out words, names, ideas. Livia said nothing. Her mind struggled to find the answer.

The answer was out there somewhere. The baby gets it. What did that mean? Nothing.

If you don't guess my name, the baby gets it. You don't get the baby.

She thought of the room downstairs, with rows of dried-up books, with all the stories from literature.

Ten seconds to go.

The answer is in the story.

The answer is in the story.

The words drummed in her head. They were all trying to speak to her. But she couldn't hear the answer.

Time had run out.

5

The man smiled. 'So sorry,' he said. 'Time is up. I do believe I hear sirens. I seem to have summoned the Pols to this very floor, where no one has been for so long. It will be interesting for them. Shame they won't appreciate it. I am so sorry that our little party was cut short. But, before you disappear, I will tell you what is in your room 101. I will tell you the thing you fear most.' He paused, his face went black, his eyes shone silver. He didn't move his lips but the words filled the room. 'What you all fear most is, of course, the death of Hope.'

Livia felt a chill run down the back of her neck. It was true. And what had her parents called her? They had called her Hope.

The face disappeared, leaving the centre of the screen blank. The square marked Security flashed at the edge. In the distance, a siren pulsed through the building.

They all looked at each other.

'We have to get out of here,' said Cassandra, looking round.

We failed after all, thought Livia, her heart sinking. And it mattered. It really mattered.

They could see where they had come in. But they

couldn't go that way. Where else? They were two hundred and fifty floors up.

They rushed over to the walls, scanning for an exit, a door, anything.

Livia glanced back at the computer. On the screen, numbers were flashing in one corner, above the word LIFTS. 99, 100, 102 . . .

A door! 'Over there!' shouted Cassandra. They ran. Opened it. Rushed in. It was only a cupboard. They were trapped! In her head, Livia was counting. The Pols would surely be at Floor 101 within a few seconds. Then a few more seconds to run along the corridor and . . . maybe a few seconds of confusion with the holograms . . .

They had failed. This was the end. No one would ever even know what had happened to them. They would be forgotten. Like dust. Handfuls of dust and splinters of bone.

'Quick! Here!' Marcus had found something. A sliding door. Stiff with lack of use, it squeaked as they forced it aside. It wasn't a cupboard after all − it was the delivery room. Connected to the service chutes where they had entered the building. But they were now two hundred and fifty floors up. Cold air rushed from the gaping blackness of two openings.

Voices, shouting. No time to lose. They climbed up onto one ledge. There was a familiar mesh basket, swaying slightly, suspended from a wire that looked much too thin.

'Come on!' said Cassandra. And the four of them clambered in. Marcus stretched his arm outside and hit the down button. Slowly at first, but gathering speed, the basket fell into the sickening drop.

Cold dusty air rushed past their faces, taking their breath away. Their eyes were forced shut and they clutched each other in terror.

They felt as though they were falling for ever but it was probably only a few seconds before they heard noise from far above, voices, shouting. They didn't look up. The basket lurched to a crashing halt and the four of them fell against each other. Livia felt a sickening pain in her back. Cassandra's head hit the side and she collapsed to her knees, groaning.

A twang. Another. They were shooting! The bullets were ricocheting off the sides of the lift shaft.

'The ladder! Get on the ladder!' Marcus was pointing to the service ladder. They squeezed through the narrow gap at the side of the basket and scrambled onto it, Tavius helping Cassandra, who was shaking her head dizzily. More twangs of bullets.

Livia closed her eyes, held her breath, as though this would make her invisible. She had to have hope.

With panic trying to choke her, she tried not to think

of the black void below. She had no idea how many floors they had dropped in the wire basket. She focused desperately on the steady movement of hands and feet as she climbed as quickly as she could down the ladder. She must not miss a step.

No more bullets. Silence. What was happening? She tried to work out what the Pols would do. Where would they be now?

Her muscles ached. The skin on her hands was raw. Each breath scraped through her lungs. Exhaustion and dizziness began to ebb over her. A numbness crept and began to blur the edges of her fear. She could give up. Stop fighting.

No! She must keep thinking. Think! What should they do? They must do what the Pols would not expect. What would they not expect?

'Stop!' she hissed. Marcus trod on her hands before he stopped. 'Cass! Tav!' Stop!'

'What is it?' said Cass. 'We can't stop!'

'We're not thinking. They know we're going down. They'll be waiting at the bottom.'

'Shit!' said Cassandra. 'You're right. We're not thinking.'

'So what do you suggest?' asked Tavius.

'We go up,' said Livia. There was a silence, but they knew she was right.

6

Without speaking, they began to climb. But Livia was thinking. A new clarity was creeping through her mind. They couldn't just keep running away. They had to go back to Floor 101 and they had to find the password.

Guess my name or the baby gets it. The computer was programmed with stories. It knew *Nineteen Eighty-four, Alice Through the Looking Glass, The Wizard of Oz, Moby Dick*. Presumably many many more. Perhaps every story ever told. So, what story fits? Guess my name or the baby gets it. Or you don't get the baby.

Guess my name or . . .

. . . you don't get the baby.

Yes! Yes! She had got it! She knew the password. It had to be!

Her heart sang. She wanted to shout.

Soon they came to the opening onto the floor. They scrambled off the ladder. Cass had a raw red scrape on her cheekbone, where a few tiny beads of blood swelled up.

'Hurry!' said Livia. She didn't want to tell the others, in case she was wrong. But she knew she wasn't. She went first, holding the gun in front of her, her heart pounding. They all pulled their hoods on and replaced the sunshades, just in case.

The room, some sort of dining area, was empty. Discarded food cartons littered the tables and floor. The Pols had obviously all left quickly. In the corridor, they found the lifts. They were at Floor 210.

'Can we assume the Pols are all at the bottom?' asked Cass.

'We have to,' said Livia, her voice tight.

'You OK, Liv?' asked Marcus.

'Yeah, totally OK!' She couldn't see his eyes behind the shades. She wished she could see them.

Into the lift. Tavius took the dead finger from his chest pocket, placed it on the pad. Pressed 101. The lift shot upwards. They said nothing while they waited. It swished to a halt. They ran along the corridor, straight into the control room. Past the holograms.

Following Livia, they rushed across the room, behind the glass wall.

Livia sat down in front of the computer screen. The man's face reappeared. 'Oh, you again,' he said. 'You came back. How delightful. But remember, we can't get very far without the password.'

'Rumpelstiltskin! Your name is Rumpelstiltskin!'

Immediately the man's face became furious as it swirled into a cartoon figure of a pointy-toed man. The word 'Welcome!' filled the screen as the little man stamped his heel so hard that it smashed right through the floor and he danced away into the distance clutching his foot.

'Brilliant, Liv!' they all said excitedly, gathering round her. Now the screen formed itself into small sections. She read LANGUAGE CENTER, SECURITY, ENTERTAINMENT, GOVERNATORS, TECH, BABY-PROG, MEDICAL . . .

'Try that box – the one that says, VIEW CAMERAS,' said Cassandra. They were all crowding round, trying to understand all the boxes on the screen.

Now they could see squares numbered 1–249. Livia pressed several in turn. Some floors showed empty corridors and desks. The workers had gone home for the night. Others showed Pols lounging in recreation rooms, or sleeping in bunks, or eating in canteens. There was an air of aimlessness.

'I want to see the floors we couldn't see into on the way up,' said Livia.

Floor 240 was empty, in near darkness. There was something like a huge reception desk, without a receptionist. At the bottom of the screen was the word GOVERNATORS. Floor 241 contained desks. Several men and women appeared to have fallen asleep at their work. Again, near darkness. Floor 242 contained a library. Six people asleep in chairs or with their faces in their books. Floor 243 consisted of armchairs around a cold fire. Most of the armchairs contained people. All asleep. Floor 244, empty chairs and empty tables. A man lying on the ground. Floor 245 looked like a small hospital ward. The patients were sleeping. Two nurses slept at their desk. A woman sprawled across a trolley. Bottles were strewn across the floor. Floor 246 contained dining-tables, with all the diners asleep in their food, or with their chins resting on their chests. Floor 247 was a kitchen. Chefs slumped across tables, food was spilt on the floor, fruit sat in baskets, apparently in perfect condition. What was going on? Every room was silent and dark, lit only by the dim yellowy night coming through the windows. At the bottom of each screen was the word GOVERNATORS.

Floor 248. Completely empty. Floor 249 the same. Floor 101 had no camera.

'What's happened to them?' whispered Cassandra. 'It's as if they've all fallen asleep in one moment, all at the same time.'

'It's like *Sleeping Beauty!*'

'Or *The Midwich Cuckoos.*'

'We'd better hope it's *Sleeping Beauty* then, hadn't we? You know what happened in *The Midwich Cuckoos.*'

'There are probably other stories where people fall asleep like that.'

'If those sleeping people are the Governators, who's in charge?'

'It's the computers!' said Tavius in awe. 'Computers have taken over! You remember what he said – that the last human who had come here was years ago. He said "The last human who had any control." '

'It's what people in the old days used to fear,' said Marcus. 'That if computers ever learnt to think and feel like humans they would end up being cleverer.'

'No!' said Livia. 'They're not cleverer!'

'Clever enough! Clever enough to take over. Don't you see? The computer is doing everything – it's making all the rules! And no one even realises. Everyone thinks the City is governed by the Governators, but it's not,' said Tavius.

'No, don't YOU see?' exclaimed Livia, excitedly. 'Humans *are* cleverer. We wrote the language! We programmed it!' Her eyes were shining. She understood at last. 'Well, not literally us, of course. Years ago, back in the twenty first century, when people taught computers really to think like humans, don't you see what they did? In order to give them real language, they inserted all the stories that had ever been written into the language program. Computers can only do what they are programmed to do. That was always true. But now they have been programmed with stories and they have been instructed to think for themselves – but because they only know stories, that's how they think. They can only act on what is programmed into them. They don't have free will. They only have stories. And that's not enough.'

Cassandra spoke. 'But amongst all those thousands of stories, how does the computer decide which to act on? How does it choose which story?'

'It's like humans,' said Marcus, beginning to understand. 'It's like our genes. We have all these millions of genes, but only some get 'switched on'. It's like an almost random sequence. Something triggers one to act and it acts on another and you get a chain reaction. But with the computer it's the stories that make it act, not genes.'

'Well, we've got to change it. Somehow. We've got to, otherwise there *is* no hope. Nothing will change.'

Livia touched the box that said LANGUAGE CENTER. A menu appeared:

add
remove
view list
check current hierarchy
set new hierarchy

She selected check current hierarchy. A list appeared to the side. At the top of the list was *Nineteen Eighty-four*. She selected it and pressed remove. remove permanently? Yes. Easy! Now the top story was *Brave New World*. They should have guessed. The funk! The dulled happiness of the Citizens! Two stories with hopeless, defeated endings. Exactly the two stories you would not want to be ruling your life. Livia selected it and pressed remove. remove permanently? Yes.

The next two stories she didn't recognise. How could she know if they had a sad ending or not? She saw a box which said voice option. She pressed it and spoke aloud: 'Select all sad stories'. The screen showed the words, 'what is a sad story? hah hah!'

She knew what she had to do. There was no time for anything else. 'Select all stories,' she said. She then selected remove. remove permanently? Yes. all stories removed.

Now she needed to reprogram it with the right stories.

She pressed add, then select story. Up came the words, no stories available for selection. no stories exist. She could see the ghostly outlines of the titles of all the stories which no longer existed. She had destroyed them all. What had she done! Why hadn't she stopped to think? She had destroyed their last hope.

A red light started to flash at the corner of the screen. The box labelled 'Security' had appeared. But when she tried to select it, all that happened was that these words appeared: complete current action. select story.

But there were no stories! She was sweating, her hands clammy. Her eyes would not work properly. 'Come on, think!' she said aloud. There's always hope!

She knew what story she wanted. The story of Pandora's box, where only hope was left after every evil filled the world. She scrolled down the faint list of deleted stories, past halfway and there it was. *Pandora's Box*. But she couldn't select it any more. She kept pressing it, as though by force she could make the computer act.

How long before the Pols realised they were not going all the way down the building? How long till they realised where they were?

7

Then Livia knew what she had to do. Trying to ignore the flashing lights, the distant sirens, her fear, she touched create. Up came a blank page. tell story, she read. She pressed voice option again and, as she began to speak, the words appeared on the screen.

'Once upon a time, once upon a time . . .' and as she struggled to find the words to create the story they needed, they came to her from her childhood. The words the Poet had told them over and over again, so that they would for ever remember who they were.

Once upon a time, in a faraway neverland, lived a beautiful princess. Her hair was as long as the sound of honey. Her skin was cake-warm. She smelt of biscuit and caramel and her eyes were lemonade bright. One day, a butterfly, its wings as blue as the sound of sadness, landed gently on her shoulder. 'O princess,' it whispered, its voice as light as a spider's breath, 'I have some terrible news for you.'

'Tell me your terrible news, O butterfly,' sang the princess, as she stroked his wings with cloud-soft fingers.

'Hope is dead. I have searched the world, O

princess,' replied the butterfly. 'I have searched high and low, the murky depths of the deepest ocean and the dizzy peaks of the highest mountain, the furthest sands of the hottest deserts and the iciest reaches of the frozen poles, and I cannot find hope. Hope is dead, O princess. Quite dead.' And the butterfly shivered as it cried in the cold empty air.

The princess smiled again. 'Do not fear, gentle butterfly. I have a secret. I am going to have a baby. And in my baby lie all my hopes, all the hopes of the whole wide world. And you will see that we will all live happily ever after because that is the way we will make it be.'

Not knowing how much longer they had, she touched enter and the story disappeared into the computer. Up came the words, choose title. She said, '*The Princess and the Butterfly*,' pressed enter, and breathed in relief as the title appeared as the only story in the computer.

What now? What had changed?

In the distance the sirens still sounded. Along the top of the screen, 'Security' was still flashing. Marcus leant across Livia and touched it. The other sections shrank into the sides of the screen and a list appeared. At the top of the list were the words SECURITY ALERT. Next to it flashed in red the words ACTIVATED – RED

ALERT FLOOR 101. Below this were the words, DEACTIVATE SECURITY ALERT. Livia touched it and the siren died away.

But still the voices, still the Pols were coming. They were already in the room. Even though the alert was deactivated, they would still see them.

'Look!' whispered Marcus. Instruct Security. Do it, Liv, quick!'

She touched the words and up came, speak new instructions. computer will transmit instructions directly to operators.

'Do not use weapons!' Livia said quickly, urgently, her mouth dry as paper. 'Weapons are now forbidden against any human. And all forms of violence,' she added quickly, just in case. 'And imprisonment. Outsiders have the same rights and access to medicine and food and jobs and help as Citizens and there will be free elec . . .'

Two Pols walked round the screen, stopped when they saw them. Livia quickly touched enter on the screen.

'What's happening, officer?' asked one of them, looking at Tavius, while also touching his ear-piece. Both Pols were listening to their ear-pieces.

There was a silence. Livia's legs felt weak.

'Er, all under control,' replied Tavius. 'False alarm.'

'False alarm, sir,' snapped the Pol who had spoken. 'Remember your rank, officer.'

'Yes, sir, sorry, sir.'

'Why you here, but? Access to Floor 101 is strictly forbidden. You know that.'

'Orders,' said Livia, hurriedly. 'Sir. We were only following orders.'

He looked at her. She was glad of her dark glasses. She hoped he could not see what she was feeling. 'Yes, well, good work, officers,' he said. His eyes followed the line of her body in its tight suit. She turned her eyes away.

I hate you. All of you. Following orders! How pathetic. Can't you even think for yourselves? Well, we give the orders now.

I would kill you if I could. Blood will have blood.

You would kill me if you knew. You killed Cass's friend. You killed my parents. You are the lowest of the low.

You should think for yourselves. You should do what is right.

But you can't *write your own story, can you? You have no power.*

'We should be going, sir,' said Cassandra.

'Yes, well, good work.' The Pol saluted them and they did their best to imitate the salute back. Had it been

264

correct? As they walked away, they felt the Pols' eyes on them. Livia forced herself to walk slowly. She wanted to run.

'Wait!' The voice echoed through the space between them. They stopped, turned. Not now! Not when they were so close to safety.

'You're not wearing your com-pieces, but.'

What? Livia's brain spun. Cass whispered to them, 'He means the ear-pieces, for messages.' Then she spoke to the Pols. 'Sorry sir. We were off duty when the alert came.'

'You don't know the new orders, so. You can't shoot Outsiders now, see? Or do anything else violent to them. Except in self-defence, just.' He smiled nastily. 'Oh, and something about Outsiders being equal – weird but, like, that's the orders, see?'

'Thank you, sir,' said Cassandra. They turned and walked away.

Into the lift. Keyed in 0. Felt the lift shoot downwards. They smiled at each other. They had done it! They wanted to laugh and shout. But they would have to wait, just a while longer.

'Look!' said Livia, pointing through the glass of the lift. As they rushed past the upper levels, they could see the floors which had been in darkness. Now they were brightly lit. The Governators had woken up. They could see, flashing past in a blur, dozens of men and women stretching and moving. As though they had just been asleep for the night.

Some seconds later, before they had had a chance to wonder at what was happening, they were at the bottom. No Pols in the foyer – they would probably be moving round from the back of the building where the lifts were.

The four of them simply walked out. It was as easy as that. The thick glass doors swished open and they walked into the floodlit night at the front of the building. Not daring to speak, they hurried away. A few people wandered past, though it was by now the middle of the night. Livia looked up and saw the time projected across the sky. It was one o'clock in the morning. It seemed later. Her eyes felt suddenly tired. Her legs were heavy and her head floated. They hadn't eaten for hours. All the emotion, the fear, swam through her, as though now at last she was allowed to feel it.

She wanted to run and scream and laugh and cry. She wanted to tell everyone what they had done. But who would understand up here? They needed to get back to the others first. Back underground with their own people.

'Let's get these clothes off,' said Cassandra. 'I hate

them. I hate what they stand for.' Around a corner, once they had made sure no one was near, they peeled off the black suits, leaving only their own clothes below. Even though the air was, as always, blood temperature, Livia shivered. But she was glad to shiver. It felt real.

Their feet were now bare against the ground. They had left their shoes behind. It didn't matter: the streets were clean.

Livia put the gun in the waistband of her leggings. She couldn't have said why.

They threw the black bodysuits in a bin and began to walk, following signs back to the solatrains.

It started to rain.

'Must be the first day of the month!' said Tavius. He was holding Cassandra's hand, Livia noticed with a smile. She looked at Marcus out of the corner of her eye. He was looking straight ahead. She kept her hands by her sides. It was like eating a piece of cake – she would always keep the icing till last, and play with it, tantalising herself till the last minute. And then she would eat the icing as slowly as possible.

'Wonder what the Governators will do about the weather now,' said Cassandra.

'Who cares?' asked Tavius. 'At least they are human. If someone's got to decide the weather, I'd rather it was a human than a computer. It's actually quite useful to know when it's going to rain. I think I fancy staying here if it's going to be like that.'

'No way,' said Livia. 'I don't want to know when it's going to rain. I want to wonder about things like that.' And as she raised her hands to wipe the damp hair from her eyes, she felt Marcus catch her fingers and hold them and the feeling was electric.

And when they looked at each other, with the tiniest smile, it was as if suddenly their thoughts met. There was no room for doubt or games any more. Desire rushed through her like a wave on shingle.

But first, they must get home.

In the solatrain, the four of them sat in silence, deep inside their own heads, exhausted, and lulled by the calming banana scent. Their shoulders were pressed together and they felt each other's breathing. Livia and Marcus still entwined their fingers and she could smell his warmth. They were all ignored by the groups of Citizens returning from their night of entertainment. No one even noticed that they had bare feet. Or if they did, they didn't care.

We must look like wrecks. There's probably still blood in my hair. But they couldn't care less.

I wonder how things will change for the Citizens. The

Governators won't be able to change everything immediately. But we put hope back into the story.

I think my parents would have been proud of me. How different I sound! Where's that anger? Where's all that pain stuff gone?

Now, if they were here, I wouldn't ask them why they gave me away. I would just say, 'Here I am. This is what I did.'

That is how much things have changed.

But I am still me.

When they left the solatrain they walked slowly to the walkways, arms linked, too tired to talk. Along the maze of white-lit glass tubes, down towards street level.

Livia's ankle began to throb, the first time she had noticed it since they had left the underground that evening.

'Is the canal near here?' asked Tavius. 'I'd like to see the water.'

'Sure,' said Cass. 'I'm not ready to go back yet either.' And she led the way down a narrow street. They could hear the lapping of the water before they saw it. The canal stretched inky-black into the distance, pebbled with rippling reflections of countless lights. Towards the other side a black shape shot past – a waterkab. On the far bank the moonscrapers stretched into the sky, their windows twinkling. Livia longed to see the stars again.

She longed for home. She felt Marcus' hand firm in hers. She wanted never to let it go. Wanted only to feel him.

They all walked slowly along the canal bank. Breathing in the different air. A milky moon hung between two moonscrapers.

Marcus turned to Livia. He pulled her to him, wrapped his arms around her back, and she smelt his skin as at last his lips met hers. As every part of her body dissolved into their kiss, she felt an emotion so strong that she could have cried or laughed and not known the difference. She thought of nothing but this and simply melted.

Neither of them heard the others cough. Neither of them heard the tiny click of a gun being unlocked nearby. Neither of them heard the first word the man spoke.

They both heard the next words.

'I said, freeze. You two – separate.'

8

Slowly, they separated. Very slowly, they swivelled their eyes around. Tavius and Cassandra were standing stone-still, staring at the corner. A Pol stood there. Only five metres away, his gun pointing straight towards them, moving from one to the other. The top of his bodysuit was pulled back. No shades. Small eyes. He smiled, as he spoke again. 'How cute. Shame it had to end, but.'

But he could not shoot them! What about the new orders? And then, with horror, Livia realised. He was not wearing his ear-piece. He had not received the new orders.

She tried to speak, 'But you can't . . .'

'Oh, I can, but. I can! I am allowed. Why should I spare you? You are vermin. You are thiefs. Like, you make our City dirty. You are trash.'

'But . . .!'

'Shut up!' he screeched. 'See you are making me angry! I came here for a quiet bit of funk and look what happens! Before I take it even, you trash spoil it all, you do.' His eyes flicked from one of them to another.

Livia moved her hand very, very slowly towards her waistband, where the gun was.

'Don't move!' the Pol shouted. She saw him tense his

finger. There was no time to think. Quick as a snake she pulled the gun out and fired. She missed. There was a cry from Tavius behind her. A splash. Blank panic. She fired again. The Pol was flung backwards by her bullet, crashing to the ground. Blood spread, black in the night, across his chest. She ran to him. His glazed eyes were dead already.

She turned. Cassandra and Marcus were shouting, 'Tav!' He couldn't swim well, never had been able to. It had always been a joke. It wasn't funny now. She ran to the edge of the canal. Just a swirl of water. No no no no! Her thoughts smashed together. She could not, would not believe this. Not now! If only she hadn't missed the first time! How could she live with herself? And if she hadn't been so wrapped up in her kiss with Marcus.

No no no no no NO!

Cassandra and Marcus both dived in. They came up spluttering. Dived down again. And again. Each time they surfaced, they gasped desperately for air. The inky water churned with their bodies. How long had Tav been down there?

There were no words in Livia's head, only dumb unbreathing panic.

The water churned again. Cassandra's head broke the surface. Her face told it all: she had not found him. She gulped at the air, preparing to go down again. But now

Marcus came up. With Tavius. His eyes were shut, his shoulders limp, his head lolling back against Marcus' arm.

Still no words, no thoughts, only chaos, and pictures as though in a film. Not real. Surely not real. More like a story, a play, where everything was acting.

Cass and Marcus swam with him to the edge and Livia leant over to help drag him up. They struggled out of the water, not speaking. Tavius lay face down and still.

Livia hit him on the back. Hard. Pressed down with the heels of her hands. Nothing. Panic exploded in her head. No! The others joined her. Marcus picked him up at the waist, used the weight of Tav's body against his hands to try to force water from him. Suddenly, Tav choked and heaved and a gush of water flooded from his mouth. He began to splutter. And opened his eyes.

As Tavius lay gasping and coughing on the bank, relief flooded over Livia. Words and thoughts came back and the chaos, the utter panic, began to fade. But where had the Pol shot him?

'Where were you hit, Tav?' she asked, looking all over him quickly, searching for blood. But it was impossible to see, with all the water and the darkness.

'Not shot. Fell. Too near edge,' he replied, still coughing.

'Bloody faker!' said Marcus, wiping the water from his face, gasping for breath. 'Remind me to teach you to swim properly when we get home!'

They helped Tav to his feet, all wanting to touch him, to know that he was alive. But they must hurry. There could be other Pols around. The city now seemed as sinister as it always had before.

Shivering now in their wet clothes, and no longer in the mood to linger, they tipped the Pol's body into the canal, and hurried back towards the safety of underground. Livia kept the gun until they reached the grating, then she dropped it down a drain and listened as it fell into the water below.

Part Six

A Death

Weave a circle round him thrice
And close your eyes with holy dread
For he on honeydew hath fed
And drunk the milk of paradise

Kubla Khan by
Samuel Taylor Coleridge

1

When they entered the underground hall again, with Tavius still coughing the water he had inhaled, there was something happening. People were standing or sitting in hushed groups and the fires were lit. Why weren't they all asleep? As soon as the four of them walked in, Helen hurried up to them. 'Quick!' she said to Cassandra. 'It's your father.'

'No!' cried Cassandra. 'No!'

They hurried towards the middle of the hall. Fire and candlelight sent a ghostly glow over everything, creating strange shadows on faces, familiar faces now. Milton's bed had been moved into the hall, near the fire for warmth. The people who stood around him moved aside as Cassandra and the others came in. She rushed to him and took his hand. Speechless, she stared and stared at his face as though by simply wishing it she could make this not happen. She touched his forehead, brushed some damp hair away. His skin was stretched over bones that seemed more hollow than even a few hours before.

He did not open his eyes. His chest rose and fell in shallow fluttering movements, with a rattle from deep within. A grey-blue haze tinged his lips.

'Father,' she whispered at last. 'I'm here. We're all here. The Pols can't shoot us any more. We're safe!' Someone put a blanket around Cass's wet shoulders. She looked exhausted.

Milton's lips moved. His voice was a tiny whisper, the words slow, with long pauses between. 'Safe . . . good . . . but not . . . every . . . thing. Are we . . . free?'

'Yes, we are free. Everything will be different now. You'll see. We changed the ending. The saddest story in the universe. It's gone.'

He was trying to speak again but his voice was so weak it was almost not there.

'Livi . . .' Livia went to the other side of the bed and took his other hand. His fingers seemed as though they might snap. She felt a slight squeeze.

She spoke to him, her words coming out in a rush before it was too late. 'You were right and wrong. About everything being in the story. It *was*, but that wasn't the important bit. It's the story we write ourselves that's important. And it's stories and language that give us the power to do that.'

He smiled. 'Your . . . mother . . . father . . . proud . . . you.'

Yes, they would. But, really, I don't need to know any more.
And I don't need to ask you now. Whether they loved me.
Whether they hurt when-they gave me up. It would just be a
story of the past. It wouldn't change who I am because I
wouldn't let it. I wouldn't write my story that way.

It won't hurt any more. It is just a part of me. A part of my
story. I will store it and then I will just build my own from it.

Milton was trying to speak. They all turned towards him. His eyes were open now, as though straining to see through the dark, glassily. 'This. Read . . .' he whispered. He pulled his hand from Cass's and tried to move it towards his head.

What did he want?

His hand fumbled at the pillow. Under the pillow. Cass helped him. She pulled out a letter.

'It has your name on it, Liv. Father?'

'Livia,' he said, summoning his last strength. 'What did . . . Poet . . . tell . . . ? About . . . parents?'

At first, Livia was too confused to answer. What was this? She felt her heart begin to beat faster. She took a deep breath and tried to speak calmly, aware of everyone watching her. 'They gave me away,' she said, her voice level. 'And then they died. Shot by the Pols.' She heard a slight intake of breath from Marcus and Tavius. She let go of Milton and took Marcus' hand.

'Not . . . true,' whispered Milton.

Not true! So the Poet had lied again! No!

'What do you mean, not true?' She must have misheard.

But Milton's eyes were closed now. His breathing was even shallower. His fingers brushed the letter still in Cass's hand. Hesitantly, Cass passed it to Livia. Livia looked at it. She didn't want to open it.

'Open,' breathed Milton, his voice now so tiny it could barely be heard.

She began to untie the string from the letter. Unfolded the thick outer paper. Inside was another piece of paper, also tied with string. Fumbling, she opened it too, dropping the outer one. She spread it out. It was dated over sixteen years before. But as she saw the first words, her eyes blurred. '*My darling Hope*,' and she could read no more.

Marcus said, 'Shall I read it?' Livia shook her head. She must do it.

As she reached the end, she felt weak, the strength draining from her stomach and her legs, her head buzzing. It could not be true. A trick. A lie. A dream.

Nothing made sense.

'It can't be true!'

'What is it, Liv?' asked Marcus gently. 'What does it say?' She passed it to him.

'Read it out,' she said. She needed to hear it again. She needed to take it in properly.

He read, frowning, as if he could not understand the words on the paper.

'My darling Hope,

'I have known you for two short weeks and you will not remember me but I will never forget you. I don't know when you will read this letter. I am giving it to Milton to keep safe. When you are old enough, he will make sure you get it.

'The Poet probably told you a story about Ten and Merrilee. The Poet didn't know that it was just that – a story. I told Milton never to tell him who you really were. So Milton agreed to make up a story about you being smuggled from hospital by two people called Ten and Merrilee. They did not exist. It was Milton's story.'

They looked at Milton. He was trying to speak. Into their silence came the words, 'Beautiful story.'

Marcus carried on reading. *'Now, I am writing the truth. Not a story. You are my daughter and I love you. One day, I hope you will know how much.*

'There is plague amongst us again and I am frightened for you. Yesterday my best friend died

with her dead baby at her side. But today Milton has come from the Poet. He is looking for babies, orphans, any babies, to save them. He has promised a good life for them and the hope of a future. What choice do I have? I have asked Milton to take you to the Poet but never, never to tell him who you are. One day, you might tell him yourself.

'You see, I never told him I was pregnant. I was too angry . . . but I have got ahead of myself. First I need to tell you who your father is. You may have guessed by now. Your father is the Poet.

Hearing it, hearing the words spoken aloud now, Livia could hardly breathe. The floor under her feet was sinking into softness.

She was barely aware of the astonishment on the faces of her friends. Marcus was still reading.

'I was in love with him. I still am. We were even going to marry. But then along came his plan – his Big Idea. He had no time for me. He was obsessed. I told him it was stupid. We had a huge row, and said things we should never have said, and that was it. After he went to Balmoral, I never saw him again. Soon afterwards, I found I was pregnant. I never told him because – oh, lots of reasons. I was still angry, I wanted you for myself, I thought I'd be a good enough parent on my own. Then the plague came, and you

282

were born, and everything is confusing now. But one thing I know is that I want to you to live and be safe and happy. So when Milton came today, it was a chance that was too good to miss. You'll be brought up by your father but he will never know.

I know you will wonder why I don't want him to know. It's because I don't know how he will react. He might reject you, might be furious with me for not telling him. Maybe also I don't want him to have what I can't. I have only been a mother for two weeks. He will have you for ever. Maybe I'm too angry, too selfish, to give him that.

I still don't care about the plan. I am not giving you to him so that you can change the world. I simply love you. I am only your mother and I can look no further than the softness of your skin.

I don't have much time. Milton is taking you now. I can't do this bit. I can't bear that I don't know what will happen to you, that I might never see you again, that the future is a blur. But I have to do it. I have to let you go.

I love you, Hope.

As much as the stars in the sky and the bubbles in a sea of champagne.

As much as the ripples of sand in a desert storm and the petals in a rose tornado.

More than the souls that have been and the souls that will be.

More than all the ideas ever thought and all the thoughts never spoken.

I told Milton that. I told him to put it in the story somewhere. I hope he remembers. It's the bit that's true. There's always a part that's true in every story. I don't know if the Poet will tell you that bit, so I'm telling you now. He taught me to make poetry, you know, the Poet did. Just in my head. For myself, and now for you.

With love for always,

Your mother,

Rose.'

Marcus stopped. He stared at the paper as though it could tell him something more. No one spoke. Livia found herself sitting in a chair. The only sound was Milton's tiny wheezing, but that had become part of everything now and she didn't hear it.

I can't think straight. What does this mean?

He doesn't know! The Poet doesn't know! He brought me up and he didn't know who I was. I thought he knew everything. But he was as much in the dark as I was.

It's the oldest story in the book. The orphan finds that the person who has looked after her all her life is her parent after all.

Does this new story change who I am?

I am grasping something but I don't know what it is.

Something is happening. If my brain could stop rocking on the waves, maybe I could catch it.

She heard a gasp from Cassandra. She turned her head and saw Milton's chest rise and fall one last time, his lips soft. The wheezing rattle died away and his body sank down and down into itself. Now, at last, it was still. Milton was dead.

Cassandra's eyes were wet. Tavius put his hands on her shoulders.

'At least he knew, Cass. He knew what we did.'

She didn't speak. Only gently closed her father's eyes.

Helen knelt at Cass's side and touched her arm. 'We will leave you for a while, Cass. Your father was proud of you. I am, too.'

The others slowly left the bed. On her way, Livia touched Cass's shoulder.

'I'm sorry,' she said. Cass nodded. She was shivering under her blanket.

Marcus still had the letter. He picked up the outer wrapper from the floor.

Sol and Helen came towards them with mugs of tea. Slices of bread and cheese.

Livia shook her head.

'You should eat, Liv,' said Tavius. 'We all should.' His face looked ill, his cough still rattling. His wet clothes were stuck to his body.

She shook her head again but Marcus took her arm and the three of them went over to some chairs near a fire. She was not properly aware of her surroundings. Her brain was filtering the wrong information. The constant background sounds of coughing and moaning and the distant dripping suddenly seemed loud and strangely important, but the voices of her friends faded and her own words were stuck somewhere tangled. She could barely remember how to move her feet one in front of the other. The ground beneath her wobbled and the skin of the water she walked on felt ready to burst.

She slumped in a chair, her mind dulled. People came and went around her. She did not speak.

I had worked it all out.

Who am I now? If I have a different story, am I a different person?

Surely, suddenly, this is not Odysseus' ship any more.

As they sat, drained of energy, Livia felt the heat of the mug in her hands and it began to bring her back to reality. Marcus and Tavius had taken off their wet clothes and someone had brought them clean trousers and shirts. Someone else brought all three of them blankets and they sat huddled in them, as the fire began to warm them through.

Marcus spoke. 'Why didn't you ever tell us, Liv — what the Poet said? About your parents.'

'I'm sorry. I felt . . .' What? Ashamed? Deserted? Unloved. She didn't feel that now.

And then a sudden thought. Like light. She put the mug down. 'My mother! She could still be alive! She must be! She . . . we could . . .' Marcus took her hands.

'No, Liv. She's not.'

'How do you know? She could easily have survived the plague. She could . . .'

'No, Liv. Your mother is dead. Look.' He passed her a piece of paper. The outer wrapper from the letter. He still held one of her hands.

A few words. Fading ink.

Dear Milton,

I have sad news for you. Rose died this morning, peacefully, after a short illness, as the saying goes. She knew she was dying and she said you would want to know. She never did go back to being a nurse, you know. She said she couldn't go back to working in the Medicenter after she gave Hope to you, so she stayed with us. She was a good woman, and we will miss her.

With all good wishes,

WW.

The date made Livia five years old. Her mother had lived five years after her birth. And in a moment of clarity, Livia realised what it all meant. All the pieces now.

'It's just another story, isn't it?' she said, her eyes wide.

'No, Liv, this one's true.'

'No, you don't see what I mean. It's a story. A true story or not – it doesn't matter. Whether it happened like this or whether it really was the story Milton made up, or something else entirely, it doesn't alter who I am now, does it? There's the bit that is me and always was, the bit I remember through all the stories, the bit that holds it all together. It's the *I* in *I remember* and *I think* and *I feel* and *I am*. It's still Odysseus' ship because Odysseus is still there. The stories are planks of wood. You do need some but you can choose which ones. You can even choose their meaning.'

'Yeah, well, one day, perhaps you can explain it so that I can understand,' said Marcus. 'Me, I'm too shattered to work it out. I can't believe we did what we did tonight, eh, Tav? We were pretty damn amazing.' And he leaned back in his chair and closed his eyes, a satisfied smile on his face, his hair tangled round his head like a lion's mane.

It's a story from the past. It can sit inside me and become a part of me. But the story that matters most is the story of the future, the one we write ourselves. It's what we do now that counts. Nothing else matters. In some weird and wonderful way, stories do mould who we are, but we can't let them control us. We control the stories. And that is what it is to be human.

I was like Dorothy, searching for understanding.

Later, lying in bed, listening to Marcus sleeping beside her, feeling and needing and loving his closeness, she touched her wrist gently. Rubbed her earlobe softly. Smelt a sudden whisper of honeysuckle. And simply smiled in the night before she slept.

Part Seven

A New Story

How beauteous mankind is! O brave new world,
That has such people in't.
        The Tempest by William Shakespeare

1

The next day, they slept all morning. When they woke
and had washed and eaten, everyone wanted to know
what had happened in Center Tower. There was
excitement that the Pols could not shoot them any
more. But there was argument too. What would the
Governators do now? How would anything change?
Why didn't the Outsiders try to take over completely,
run the City themselves? Surely their work was not
finished? Perhaps, even, it had only just begun.

Some complained that the future was still uncertain.

'What do you expect?' argued Livia. 'The future IS
uncertain. We can't have everything tied up neatly and
our future handed to us on a plate. It's not like a story.'

'We make the future ourselves,' Marcus said. 'We
decide. That's what's different now. We can all choose
what to do, where to go, who to be. We can find ways
to change anything we want to.'

'We can change it from within,' added Tavius.

'Because we're not Outsiders any more.' Tavius now was never far from Cassandra's side. She was pale and her eyes were slightly swollen, but she looked calm. At peace with herself now.

'What about the Citizens?' asked someone.

'Theirs is a different sort of happiness. Maybe we can't judge or measure someone else's happiness,' said Cass. 'Just because it doesn't seem enough for us.'

'Besides, we can't alter the way their brains work. It's the way they are. It's all they can do,' added Tavius. He had a fresh bandage on his arm and he was no longer coughing.

Helen looked at Cassandra. 'You were right,' she said. 'Well done. All of you. And . . . and I'm sorry. I didn't believe you, trust you, but I was wrong. Will . . . he would have been proud.'

In the middle of this had come the news. Some Outsiders had returned from a trip to sell moonstones, hurrying back because of what they had heard. They had been sitting outside the Medicenter, arguing as to whether they should go in and try to find medicines. People were coming out of the building and, even though the faces remained bland, there was a tiny buzz of excitement. When they had asked a Citizen what was happening, he had told them that the baby-programming unit was being 're-structured'. No babies would be de-languaged any more. None of the Citizens understood what this meant. They were all going home with new pim scrips and most of them were desperate for some funk to help them deal with the uncertainty.

Another gleam of hope.

Tavius was not going back to Balmoral. He wanted to begin to change things straightaway. He was fired with new enthusiasm and had chosen to stay. With Cassandra. 'It is a far, far better thing I do,' he had joked with his arm around her waist. He had washed and combed his hair. He looked like his old self. But different, thought Livia. Somehow different.

'Shut up, Tav!' said Marcus.

'No more quotes from stories!' said Cass. 'That's what caused the problem, remember.'

'No, that's how we solved the problem,' Livia reminded her. She looked at the two of them together and realised exactly how Tavius had changed. He had found a heart and passion. He had found his place.

Livia climbs the stairs once more towards her old room. She climbs alone. The others are downstairs. Her old friends. And Marcus. And the Poet. All look the same and different to her now. Because she is looking through the same and different eyes. Marcus is a part of her, drawn into who she is, making her heart beat differently, occupying his own place in her head. His smile is still the same. It's what it does to her that's changed. The Poet's hair is thinner, his eyes are greyer, but his old gnarled jumper still smells of her childhood. And the lurch in her heart when she sees him is new. His smile is different, too, as he grows slowly into his own new story.

Livia reaches under her bed and pulls out her old guitar. And as she gently draws her fingers across the strings she feels the first circle of her life complete and twist imperceptibly into the next one. Changing and the same. Moving from the present to the future.

Her own new story will be full of hope. Because that is the way she will write it. But she does not know what will be in it. It is not that sort of story.

Epilogue

A snake came to my water-trough one day
And I in pyjamas for the heat, to drink there
The Snake by DH Lawrence

Slowly he lowered himself onto the soft chair which fitted him perfectly. The screen hummed in front of him, awaiting his further instructions. As he leant back he allowed himself to smile. It was the smile of a man who has kept a secret dream all his life and seen it become reality.

His ancestors would be proud. After their generations of service to others, now *he* was in control. He had won and no one had even suspected he was trying. They would regret that they had ignored him. The butler was more important than any of them had dreamt.

Alone on Floor 101, the two hundred and fiftieth floor of Center Tower, he looked out over the starry City below. His City. He was King of all he surveyed. King. He rolled the delicious word around his mouth like baccy and remembered how it used to be a swearword. He whittled a stick with a small knife. His battered copy of *The Prince* lay on the table.

Everything had gone exactly according to plan. His plan.